Knight Moves
A Merriweather Sisters Time Travel Novel
Book 2

Cynthia Luhrs

Acknowledgments

Thanks to my fabulous editor, Arran at Editing720

To everyone who ever believed in fairy tales.

There was a little girl
by Henry Wadsworth Longfellow

There was a little girl,
Who had a little curl,
Right in the middle of her forehead.
When she was good,
She was very good indeed,
But when she was bad she was horrid.

Through the Looking Glass
by Lewis Carroll

...Alice laughed. "There's no use trying," she said: "one can't believe impossible things."

"I daresay you haven't had much practice," said the Queen.

"When I was your age, I always did it for half-an-hour a day.

Why, sometimes I've believed as many as six impossible things before breakfast..."

Chapter One

Present Day—Holden Beach, North Carolina

Melinda Merriweather slammed the laptop shut, making the table wobble precariously.

"Have you seen the story?"

Without waiting for Charlotte's answer, Melinda ranted, "It says—and I quote—*Simon Grey, Lord Blackford, and his American guest, Lucy Merriweather, were lost at sea after a crumbling wall at Blackford Castle gave way and they plunged to their deaths. The treacherous currents swept the bodies out to sea.*"

She arched a brow at her youngest sister, anger stretching her face tight. "What a load of horseshit. We are going back."

"No. I can't deal with seeing that desolate place again." Charlotte shivered. "It oozes sadness and heartbreak. But I can't stay here either. Everything reminds me of Lucy."

Melinda didn't want to hear the rest, but Charlotte hurried on. "So I'm leaving. But I'm not going to England. I need to get away. Far away. There's a gig in Djibouti and I'm taking it. I leave tomorrow."

How could Charlotte not want to go back? There had to be something the authorities missed. They'd flown over as soon as they were contacted about Lucy. Everything the authorities said seemed to filter in through a big ball of cotton. To lose your sister and aunt on the same day stretched Melinda's ability to concentrate to the limit.

The cops found Lucy's phone smashed on the rocks. But her purse was in the small cottage on the property, along with all her clothes. Melinda didn't think her sister would leave her purse and passport unattended. The facts made sense, yet something felt off.

A feeling was enough. Melinda was going back to England and not leaving until the feelings of wrongness went away. Lucy would've done the same for her.

Melinda opened up the laptop again and started to make plans.

What were the chances? Melinda booked the last ticket and now, two weeks later, she was ready to go. Her flight left at six tonight. Preoccupied with whom she would speak to first, she yelped when the headlights seemed to appear out of the sky. It was foggy but the idiot was almost on top of her. The horn blared; she swerved and swore. The driver kept going.

A sigh of relief whooshed out and she slumped into the seat, feeling the adrenaline leave her body. Better pay closer attention to the road.

Only a few more exits until the airport. She switched the satellite radio to eighties tunes and glanced in the rearview to see the same car. If he got any closer he'd be sitting in the backseat.

Barely resisting the urge to slam the brakes and teach the jerk a lesson, Melinda took the next exit and pulled into the right lane to let him pass. Where was everybody? It was three o'clock on a Wednesday; people should be out and about. But the road was practically deserted. She counted two cars going the opposite direction.

One second. She looked down for one second when she felt the impact. The last thing she saw was the ugly face staring at her through the windshield of the other vehicle before everything went black.

Melinda blinked slowly. Every inch of her body hurt. The smell of smoke and burning rubber made her wrinkle her nose and breathe through her mouth. As she looked to the right, she let out a squeak. The voice in her head laughed. A squeak? You do not squeak. Scream, yell, rant, rave. But never ever squeak.

The fact she was talking to herself made her worry. How badly was she injured? Trudy, her reliable, trusty car, looked like somebody had taken it and put it through a mixer. Seeing the heap of metal, Melinda sent up thanks to whoever was watching over her that she was somehow on the ground away from the car. Thank the stars she wasn't dead. Though right about now she felt like she was dead. Then again. If you were dead, likely you didn't feel anything. So a body screaming in pain was actually a good sign, right?

Shoes appeared in her line of vision. Scuffed brown boots. Followed the boots up denim-clad legs to a Peatbog Faeries t-shirt. The man possessed one of the ugliest faces she'd ever seen.

"Call 911. I think I'm dying."

The man sneered, "That's the idea, love."

Her brain registered the fact he was English. And that set off all kinds of internal alarms. Melinda tried to sit up, screamed in pain, and stopped moving. If she could stop breathing, maybe everything would stop throbbing in time to her erratic heartbeat.

"Shut up and call for help."

"Red, you should have left the country like baby sister Charlotte. Don't worry. My partner is on the way to end her. The client asked for fire, so she'll burn."

The man looked around to make sure they were alone. Why wasn't there ever a cop around when you needed one? Better yet, some comic book superhero to fly down and kick this guy's ass.

"You're wrong. I'm leaving the country. I was on my way when you smashed into me."

The man laughed. "To London. Wrong choice. You nosy Americans can't leave things alone, can you?"

An awful suspicion tried to take shape in her muddled brain. Before she could make sense of the thought, he spoke again.

"My client might be dead. Doesn't matter. I always finish the job, no matter what. He wanted you two birds taken out, so that's what will happen."

He reached behind him, hands going to his back, and Melinda found herself looking down the barrel of a gun. In the afternoon light, the patchy fog turned the black of the gun blue. And for an instant she thought it looked rather pretty. That was until she heard the sound of the safety clicking off.

"Nothing personal. Just business."

Everything seemed to slow down until there was only her watching him. She noticed his eyes narrow. The corner of his mouth tightened and a vein in his neck throbbed. Melinda fancied she could see his finger slowly squeezing the trigger. And then the world exploded into sound.

"Drop the gun!"

A sigh of relief escaped. The cops had arrived.

"Bollocks."

And in that strange way time has of slowing down, Melinda saw his mouth moving, tried to make out the words, while at the same time she heard the click of the trigger. She closed her eyes to wish the bullet away.

The noise sounded like firecrackers. Shouldn't she be dead? One eye cracked open, then the other. Beside her on the wet pavement lay the man. Eyes open and unseeing, a round red hole in the center of his forehead.

Hysteria took over: "...a little curl right in the middle of her forehead..." One of her favorite childhood poems filling her head, repeating over and over on some kind of demented loop.

Why did they have to kill him? A bullet to the leg should have stopped the guy. Now she'd never get answers.

Who was the client he worked for? He'd said his client was dead. Simon? Why would Simon want she and Charlotte dead?

Oh no, no, no. Did Simon kill Lucy and now wanted to make sure she and Charlotte didn't cause trouble? The jerk could've faked his death.

But wouldn't this guy know that? So many questions. Melinda knew one thing. If Simon wasn't dead, she was going to kill him with her bare hands.

"Miss. Stay with me." The cop turned his head, yelling over his shoulder, "We're losing her. Where's my bus?"

He took her hand in his. She felt the rough skin on his fingers rub against her palm. Kind eyes looked down at her. They were brown, like a happy cow.

"I don't want to die." As she said the words, she felt like an old-fashioned clock winding down. Her breath turned to ice deep within her chest.

The voice in her head screamed, *No! You can't die. You have to find out what happened. If you die, there won't be anyone to warn Charlotte.*

She heard muffled noises, groaned as hands lifted her onto a hard surface. Saw the roof of the ambulance and watched as the scene in front of her started to shrink in from the sides, slowly going dark.

From far below, she heard a voice. "Stay with me. Come on, we're losing her."

The scream of machines, then someone yelling, "Code blue."

Chapter Two

Melinda opened her eyes to a sea of white and an antiseptic smell. It took a few minutes to realize she was lying in a hospital bed. She tried to speak, but her throat spasmed; the words tumbled out, garbled. A hand touched hers. She looked up to see Charlotte.

"Don't try to talk. I'll get some water."

At least she was alive. Melinda tried to remember what had happened.

Charlotte must've gone to get the doctor, because a super-hot man wearing a white coat strode into the room looking very professional and busy.

"Glad you're awake."

"I need to go home." She had to get home, book another ticket, and find out what the hell was going on.

The doctor chuckled. "Let's take it easy."

His face transformed into the serious doctor look, making Melinda wonder what kind of bad news he was about to impart.

"You've been in a coma for almost five months, Mellie."

Charlotte only called her by the childhood nickname when something was really wrong or she was horribly upset.

The doctor went through his spiel while Melinda swallowed down the rising panic.

"Stop. Why can't I remember what happened? All I remember is a man purposely running me off the road."

She could almost see his face, almost hear the words as he leaned over her.

"I can't remember what he said. I know he meant me harm." She looked at Charlotte. "And you too."

"The cops said it was road rage." Charlotte rolled her eyes. "Talk about cuckoo for Cocoa Puffs."

The doctor looked sympathetic. "It's normal to experience memory loss. You're doing remarkably well, all things considered. You are one lucky woman. We'll reevaluate in a few days; run some more tests before making any determinations."

A nurse finished fussing over her, and set a tray on the table containing disgusting green Jell-O and something else unidentifiable that smelled hideous. With a wide smile, she turned and left with the doctor. Charlotte waited until they closed the door before she spoke.

"I've been here with you the whole time, Mellie. You don't now how worried I've been." Charlotte's voice wavered.

Melinda swallowed a couple times before answering. Her voice was a gravelly whisper. "Thank you for being here. I have to remember what that jerk said to me."

She paused. What was it? The accent. "I know he was English. Dammit, why can't I remember more?"

"The memory will come back in time. At least, the doctor thinks it will." Charlotte picked at her fingernail polish and wouldn't meet Melinda's eyes.

"Don't be mad, Mellie. I have to leave." Charlotte held up a hand. Melinda shut her mouth with a snap. Charlotte never showed such gumption. Her little sister was growing a backbone. Good for her.

"Don't give me that look. You don't understand. You died in the ambulance and they brought you back. I lost one sister. I can't lose another."

Charlotte took a deep breath. "There's a project deep in the Carpathian Mountains. Some kind of archaeological dig. Holden Beach just isn't the same anymore with Aunt Pittypat and Lucy gone. Everywhere I look I see sadness. You walk around like a zombie. Barely functioning at work, and you've quit smiling."

She squeezed Melinda's hand in hers and leaned over to kiss her on the cheek.

"I'll stay until they let you go home, and then I'm leaving."

One thing about her sister—she might be the free spirit of the family, but when Charlotte made up her mind, there was no changing it. Melinda knew better than to try. She wanted desperately to keep Charlotte next to her, keep her safe. But knowing she couldn't, she pushed the feelings down, managing a tiny half-smile.

"Thank you for staying with me and believing I would make it back. I thought I heard your voice calling me back from the shadows."

She looked up at her baby sister, tears in her eyes. "I swear I heard Lucy's voice too. Maybe I was dreaming; maybe it was something more. She sounded happy."

Melinda motioned Charlotte closer and whispered, "I won't nag you to death about staying if you promise to do one thing for me."

"Anything."

"I'm not staying here a few more days. I'll rest today, but tomorrow I'm outta here. I need answers. The only place I'll find them is in England. Where Lucy disappeared."

Charlotte smiled. "I'll pinky swear."

Melinda held out her pinky, letting the tears roll down her cheek as they swore the solemn oath from childhood.

Charlotte insisted on driving to the airport, claiming Melinda might still be loopy from the drugs they'd given her in the hospital. Her baby sister got out, grabbed her bags from the trunk, and hugged her. Melinda swallowed.

"Be careful. Now that the psycho is dead, we should be safe, but all the same, you're going to vampire country."

Charlotte waved a hand in the air, the stack of bracelets on her arm tinkling.

"Will you ever quit teasing me about what I read?" She hugged Melinda tight. "Be careful driving back home. Are you sure you're okay to drive?"

"I'm fine. Go."

"I thought the doc was going to stroke out when we signed you out."

"He was pretty ticked. Promise I'll take it easy. Now get going, or you'll miss your flight. I'm going home to stare at the ocean, read, and take a long nap." Melinda crossed her fingers behind her back so the lie wouldn't count.

She drove to the house, parked the car in the garage, grabbed the bags she'd stashed in the bathroom, and left the keys with a neighbor. The lady who lived next door had a son who needed a place to stay. He'd housesit while she was in England. She'd asked for two weeks' vacation and hoped it would be enough time. A horn sounded, signaling the car was waiting.

The driver stowed Melinda's bags then held the door.

"One stop before the airport."

At the cemetery, Melinda made her way down the meandering path to the Merriweather family plot.

"I know you would understand what I have to do." Melinda arranged the flowers in front of the tombstone. Aunt Pittypat would have loved the bright colors.

"I swear I will find out what happened to Lucy. Charlotte and I are out of danger, but I'll always look out for her. Promise." She blew her nose. "Wherever you are, any help you can give me from the great beyond would be greatly appreciated."

With a heavy heart, Melinda turned to her right and stared at the other shiny new headstone, the letters carved dark and deep.

So much had happened over the past seven months. Losing her sister had given Melinda the courage to dump Carl. What was it with the Merriweather sisters? They all seemed to have terrible taste in men, herself included. Even Aunt Pittypat married eight times trying to get it right. She always said men were fun but more trouble than they were worth.

Lucy used to call him a grade-A jerk. Melinda remembered how mad her sister would get at something Carl said or did. The final straw came right after she'd found out about Lucy. Melinda caught Carl in the women's bathroom at the Shiny Diner doing the nasty with the waitress. She suspected he'd been cheating on her, but didn't have proof until that moment.

If Melinda hadn't lost Lucy, would she have had the strength to kick Carl to the curb? She'd invested a lot of time with him. Working to make him into the man she wanted him to be. He'd been a rough, lumpy rock when she found him, and now he was starting to smooth out some of the rough edges. All that work down the drain.

It took months after the breakup for her to realize—you can't change a man. Or anyone, for that matter. They come in the state they are, and, in her experience, rarely changed. It was a hard lesson learned, one she would never forget.

She placed a hand on top of the tombstone. "I swear I'll find out what really happened."

The sunflowers bobbed in the breeze as if agreeing. Melinda wiped a tear away and walked to the waiting taxi.

Chapter Three

It took every last mile she'd banked over the years, but it was worth it. There was no way Melinda could deal with being scrunched together in coach until they landed in London in the morning. First class all the way, baby.

Talk about a different world. None of the other passengers made eye contact or spoke to one another. A flight attendant handed her a glass of champagne, an eye mask, and a blanket. Nice.

"Dinner will be served once we're airborne. Make your selection from the menu, and here's the dessert menu."

"Ooh, lemon cheesecake, my favorite."

The flight attendant leaned down. "It's even better with a scoop of raspberry sorbet."

"Done."

The attendant moved on. Melinda noted each person had a single seat that reclined into a bed. Good. She wanted to be left alone. Before she knew it, they were airborne and dinner was served.

She would bet a pound of country ham Simon was behind the attempt on her life. In the hospital she'd asked Charlotte if anything strange had happened, any near miss, but her sister just looked at her like she was crazy.

The English guy was dead. They were safe. No more worrying. Her only task was to find out what happened to Lucy.

For the first time ever, Melinda woke refreshed on the plane. The air smelled stale, but at least she'd been able to sleep. Breakfast was actually good. She brushed her teeth, used enough makeup to achieve that no-makeup look, and was ready to put on her private investigator hat. Hopefully between all the books she'd read and television she'd watched, Melinda would find the answers she needed.

The rental car was small enough to park anywhere. She had to laugh, reading all the warnings plastered all over the car to keep left. How many tourists crashed each year driving on the right by mistake? Getting out of the airport and onto the highway without incident made Melinda relax and enjoy the drive.

It was so cold. Sure, it got cold in North Carolina, but the cold here seemed to burrow into her skin. She turned up the heat, found a station on the radio to sing along with, and was happy it wasn't snowing. The highway gave way to smaller roads as she passed cute cottages and small villages.

Melinda stopped for fuel, ate lunch, then stopped again for caffeine. What she wouldn't give for an icy-cold sweet tea. At the next stop she finished filling the car up and yawned. According to the map, she was almost there. No matter how tired she was, no napping. She'd stay up until her usual bedtime tonight so her body would quickly acclimate to the time change.

As she drove through the village, the shell of a burned-out church stood in stark contrast to the homes around it. There were several quaint-looking shops lining both sides of the street. Up ahead she spotted Blackford pub. The car safely parked, Melinda hurried inside and almost groaned in pleasure as the warmth pushed the cold out of her bones.

A tiny table near the fire beckoned. She stretched, releasing the tension in her neck and shoulders, before sitting in the chair and letting the fire warm her.

It was half past five. There were a few folks at the bar and tables, but otherwise the place was hers. Guess the dinner rush or evening drinkers hadn't shown up yet. The quiet murmur of voices soothed her. Curious looks passed over her, followed by whispers.

She recognized the signs of a stranger in a small town. Heck, she knew everyone in Holden Beach. If someone came into French's, everyone would have whispered and talked about the stranger. That is, until beach season. Then from late April to Labor Day there were crowds, too much traffic, and noise. Ugh, it was annoying just to think about.

Melinda bet the small village of Blackford didn't have to deal with too many tourists. She ordered hot tea and a bowl of stew.

"Get you anything else, miss?"

Lucy's boyfriend might have been a jerk and a crazed murderer, but he had an accent to die for. Oops, so not funny. The bartender stood looking down at her, a smile hovering at the corners of his lips, as if he knew the effect he had on her. She resisted the urge to tell him he could be ninety and she'd look at him the same way.

"I'm good. On the way into town, I passed a church. What happened?"

He nodded to two old guys at the bar trying to get his attention. "Another pint?"

When he smiled, she found herself smiling back. He had a friendly face.

"Let me take care of these blokes and then I'll fill you in."

Melinda finished the stew and bread. The fire warmed her back, making her drowsy.

"Brought you some more tea." Mr. Too Good-looking For His Own Good sat down across from her.

"You were wanting to know about the church?"

She nodded, which was all it took for him to chat away.

"So it was passing strange. Old Father Moore hated technology. The young Father Moore tried to get him to change for years, but it never happened. A fire broke out in the storage closet, destroying everything. All the records were lost."

He looked off into the distance. "Since nothing was

computerized, records of births, deaths, marriages...all gone." He grinned at her.

"A lot of the blokes in town think it's a sign. No proof of marriage. They're thinking it's a chance to find a young bird."

"Aren't you the charmer?" She couldn't resist. Melinda stretched her foot out, caught the leg of the chair, and gave a little tap.

He fell backward, and she tried not to laugh, really she did. But the laughter bubbled up, and for the first time since Lucy went missing, Melinda laughed so hard it hurt.

"Not funny."

She bit the inside of her cheek. "Sorry. I wasn't laughing at you." She clapped a hand to her mouth to stifle the giggles. The look on his face... She clapped the other hand over her mouth.

The bartender dusted off his butt. "I've got to get back to work if you're not needing any other questions answered."

She snickered. Then held a hand up. "I'm so sorry. I can't seem to help it. Really, I don't mean to laugh at you."

Melinda took a deep breath. "I haven't laughed since my sister went missing. Lucy Merriweather."

He cocked his head. "The American?"

Melinda nodded, afraid to say anything.

"She and some bloke were poking around Blackford. A wall gave way and the sea took them. Terrible storm that night."

"Simon. The bloke was Simon. He owns the castle."

Now he looked confused. "Blackford Castle?"

"Simon Grey is Lord Blackford. Or was, until he supposedly died with my sister."

"There hasn't been a Lord Blackford since the fifteen hundreds. And they were named Brandon, not Grey."

He turned and yelled across the small room. "Griffin. When did the last Lord of Blackford die?"

The old guy scratched his nose. "Winston Brandon. He passed in 1564. The castle went to the National Trust."

Her hand trembled as she lifted the teacup. Winston was their dad's name. Okay, so it was a common enough name. But then why would Simon lie about owing a castle? Guess some guys would do anything to impress a girl.

She set the cup down, sloshing tea over the edge, suddenly tired. "Thanks for the information. I didn't notice any hotels when I drove through town. Is there someplace to stay nearby?"

He grinned at her. "You're in luck, love. We've rooms above."

"I'm not sure how long I'll be here. Maybe a few days to a couple of weeks?"

"I'll get the key and show you to your room. By the way, name's Brad if you need anything. You've lovely green eyes and that red, curly hair." He put a hand over his heart. "I think I'm in love."

"I bet you say that to all the girls." She blushed. This guy must kill it with the ladies. Nope. Not interested. After Carl, she was off men for good. The Merriweather sisters' curse of choosing bad men stopped with her. Here and now. England would be the start of new choices, better choices.

Brad brought in her luggage, carried it up a narrow stairway, and opened a door. The room was small but cute. The four-poster bed looked like she could sink into it.

"Loo is down the hall. Let the water run for a few minutes to get hot. My brother, Henry, will make you breakfast in the morning." He handed her the key. "Fancy a drink?"

"No, I'm exhausted. Got a lot of work to do before bed." She gently shut the door.

The next morning, after breakfast dressed in a sweater, leggings, and boots, Melinda was ready to face the castle again. The first time, just after Lucy fell, she hadn't really noticed much. A vague impression of stone and the ocean beyond were all she could recall.

"Heard you're headed to the castle." He pointed to the thermos at her feet. "Want some coffee to take along?"

"Tea would be great."

She pulled on her coat and a dark blue hat and scarf Lucy had crocheted for her two years ago.

"Here you are."

"Thanks. I've been drinking gallons of hot tea since I landed. It's so cold."

"Where are you from? By the accent, I'm guessing somewhere in the South."

She tucked her mittens in her pockets along with the key to her room. No need to bring anything else with her; she'd only be gone a few hours.

"North Carolina. And I was going to say you were the one with the accent."

He laughed. "Be careful and stay off the stairs. They're unstable." Henry held the door for her. "Car's warmed up."

"Thank you. And don't worry; I don't plan on climbing anything. Just need to have a look around."

"You're the sister. Sorry about what happened."

Familiar pain lanced through her. "I'll be back around lunchtime."

It was a short drive up to the castle. She had the place to herself. Melinda put the keys in the center console along with her room key, pulled on her mittens, and followed the paved path leading from the car park to the ruins.

Cold, salty air blew through her hair, pulling a curl loose from the hastily done French braid. She walked along the outer walls until she came to the North Sea. Talk about some serious surf. On the rocks she spotted wreckage. What looked like wood. Maybe from a boat? Or something that fell from the castle.

Melinda made her way through the courtyard, stopping at a stone bench. It nestled against the wall, blocking most of the wind. She sat down and looked around. This was the last place Lucy had visited. What happened to her?

A big black bird cawed from above. The raven landed on the wall to Melinda's left. They stared at each other for a long moment. The wind shifted and a stone fell, landing on her foot.

"Ow. Thanks a lot."

The raven cocked its head, looked at the ground, and, with a loud caw, flew off. She rubbed her foot. Something was in the hole left by the falling rock. Melinda leaned over and pulled out a worn piece of cloth. There was something wrapped in the wool. Slowly unwrapping the cloth, she saw what must have been paper at one time. Given the harsh sea air, the letter could have been written weeks or centuries ago.

As the breeze blew over her, the fragments scattered to the wind. One piece caught her eye, as it seemed to hover in the air just out of reach.

A drop of sweat ran down her side, her heart beat in time to the waves, and black and blue spots formed in front of her eyes. Melinda recognized that handwriting with the swirly S and the smiley face in the bottom of the letter. Her sister had done it ever since she'd learned her letters as a child. No amount of fussing by the teachers would get Lucy to change. She said S was a happy letter.

Lucy. The word on the scrap of paper was safe. Melinda reached out to grab the fragment, desperate for what might have been the last thing her sister wrote. The wind snatched it away. And as she helplessly watched, the paper tumbled end over end until it disappeared over the cliffs.

What on earth did it mean?

Chapter Four

Melinda held up her hand and frowned. The pretty coral polish was chipped and she'd broken three fingernails. No wonder, after pushing and prodding every single stone around the bench to no avail. She'd remove the polish and file her nails tonight.

Then she worked her way down the wall, following it around the castle all the way back to where she started. As she sat on the bench, Melinda pulled her hat off, letting the cold, salty air cool her down. A gust of wind snatched her hat.

"Oh, just flipping great." She jammed the scarf in her coat pocket. No way she'd lose it too.

Talk about hot and sweaty. Whoever came up with the phrase "Southern women glow instead of sweat" was insane. She sniffed at her underarm. "Phew."

"Did you just smell your armpit?"

Melinda jumped, feeling her face heat up. "You should

pretend not to see. But since you ask, yes, I did. And yes, I stink. Thank you very much."

Henry busted out laughing. He stuck his nose in the air and pursed his lips. "My apologies, princess."

"What are you doing here?"

He held up an old-fashioned basket. "You missed lunch ages ago. It will be dark in a few hours. Thought I'd better come up and check on you."

"I didn't realize how late it was getting. No wonder I'm famished."

"Want to go back down the pub or eat here?" He eyed her. "You look as if you've been crawling around in the dirt."

"Aren't you the charmer. Just like your brother. Must run in the family."

"Aye, it does, love. But I think you're immune."

"I am. Got all my shots before I crossed the pond. Let's eat here, and I'll tell you why I'm a filthy, stinking mess." Too bad she was done with men. Henry was funny and cute. Of course, they had the whole geographically undesirable thing going on. Nope. She had a job to do. No distractions. Enjoy the view, flirt a little, but nothing more.

Henry unpacked a veritable feast. He pulled out bread, fresh from the oven, homemade butter, tea in a thermos, and some kind of heavenly smelling chicken potpie, the steam wafting in the air and tickling her nose. He spread out a small cloth on the bench between them, nodded at his handiwork, then toasted her. She with tea and him with beer.

"Ah, that's good."

Melinda took a sip of the tea. "You remembered to put honey in it."

"I know how you like your tea. I'm a good bartender, remember?"

They ate in companionable silence, the sounds of the surf against the rocks calming her. Melinda wiped her mouth, sat back with a groan, and patted her stomach. "Delicious. Thank you again for bringing me lunch. I hope I didn't put you out."

"No bother. Ready to tell me why you're covered in dirt and dust?"

She looked at him for a moment. Would he think she was crazy? Who cared. She came from a long line of crazy Southern women—might as well embrace it.

"The reason I'm here is to find out what really happened to my sister. Maybe she was lost at sea, maybe not. I need to know how they fell."

Melinda took a sip of tea, thinking about how to frame what she wanted to tell him without sounding like a crazy person. After all, there was eccentric Southern crazy, and batshit crazy.

"I was sitting here on the bench when this big black bird, I think it was a raven, flew down and landed on the wall next to me. I swear the bird was trying to tell me something. He cawed and flew away, and when he did, a rock fell out of the wall. There was something in the opening. It was like the bird knew it was there and he'd just been waiting for me to get here."

Henry grinned. "Let me guess. Buried treasure? Or gold

from a pirate's booty?"

"Well, of a sort. It was a bundle wrapped in cloth. When I unwrapped it, I could tell it had been some kind of paper, maybe parchment? But it crumbled to dust as I held it. Though not before I saw writing."

She paused, knowing what she was about to say would sound like she was some New Age hippie, like her sister.

"I know the sea air can corrode and destroy almost everything it comes into contact with. So I realize the letter could've been written, what, a few weeks ago? Months ago? It looked really old. But the handwriting...it was my sister Lucy's."

Henry pursed his lips, a thoughtful look on his face. "There are tales about Blackford." He gestured toward the castle. "The old priest said your sister and her boyfriend weren't the first ones to be lost to the sea."

"What? There have been others?" Melinda jumped up and started pacing in the dirt. "I need to talk to him."

Henry shook his head. "I'm afraid that's going to be difficult. Father Moore suffered a stroke. He can't talk. Given his age, they're not sure if he'll recover."

"Oh. Sorry to hear. Is there anyone else who might know? Or maybe articles in the paper?"

He scratched his head. "Might be. My brother would know. We'll ask when we get back."

Henry stood and put a hand on her arm to stop her from pacing. "I'm sorry. If my brother died here, I'd tear the place apart looking for answers."

She looked up at him. "Thank you for not thinking I'm

crazy."

Melinda turned in a circle, thinking of all the places she could search. "I think I'll spend the few hours of daylight I have left exploring the castle."

"Then let's get started, aye?" Henry efficiently packed up the remains of their lunch, finished off his beer, and shot her a blinding smile. "Let me stow this in the boot and I'll help you search."

For the next several hours they wiggled rocks, climbed over debris, and searched for any kind of clue. Henry was right: it was faster with two people. Melinda didn't know what she hoped to find, only that she had a feeling there was something she was missing.

When they got back to the pub, they would talk to Brad. See what else he might know. Was there a serial killer on the loose? Or some shadowy group kidnapping people?

Melinda rolled her eyes. She was getting punchy. Coming up with all kinds of implausible ideas. What was the saying? The simplest explanation was usually the right one. Too bad she didn't have a simple explanation. Not one she liked.

Some of the walls were unstable, rooms ended in jagged openings, and she was afraid to climb several of the staircases. The growing darkness made her swear. Unable to see, she had to give up.

"Where's your car?"

He grinned. "I walked. Figured you'd drive me back so I didn't freeze my arse off."

The ride back to the pub was short, and she gratefully sank down next to the fire to warm herself.

"I added whiskey to your tea. To help take the chill off." Brad handed her a mug of the steaming liquid.

Melinda inhaled. "Thank you. I feel like a giant Popsicle."

The two brothers joined her around the fire, along with two of the older men Melinda had decided were permanent fixtures of the pub.

Brad pointed to the older gentleman on his left. "This is Angus." He pointed to the man sitting across from her. "And Magnus."

He grinned at her. "Yes, they're brothers."

Both men smiled at her, inquisitive blue eyes watching her behind thick glasses.

"I was hoping either of you could tell me anything you might know about people disappearing around here."

She sipped the tea, feeling the warmth spread to her stomach as the whiskey did its job. She could feel her toes again thanks to the fire. Melinda pulled the soft blanket tighter around her. Henry had brought it over for her when they arrived.

Angus spoke first. "You're the American lost her sister, yes?"

She nodded.

"Saw her come through here with some rich fop from London."

Magnus jumped in. "He was a rude one. Stepped on my toe, didn't even apologize."

"We thought she was too good for him. Sorry you lost her." Angus turned to his brother, silent communication passing between them. He turned back to her. "The old stories say they always come back."

She leaned forward in the chair. "What, like fairytales?"

Magnus nodded. "You might say that. Father Moore liked to talk about the strange happenings at the castle. He said in all his time here, one other person disappeared, a young boy. He was found six months later wandering around incoherently. He told a fantastical tale of other lands, but no one believed him."

The man shrugged and took a long pull of his drink. "Your sister might not be dead. She might be with the fairies."

Fairies. Melinda didn't know whether to laugh or to scream. There was no such thing as fairies. But she listened as they told various tales. Each one more outlandish than the next. She would bet most of the tales could be traced back to somebody being drunk.

She yawned for the third time. Brad ushered the men back to the bar.

"Sorry about them. They can get a little carried away." Henry took her teacup before it slid off her lap. "What do we do now?"

Maybe the thoughts had been swirling around her mind all this time, but suddenly Melinda knew what she was going to do.

"I'm going to check out in the morning. Head back to London and do some research on missing persons in the area. I don't know what I'll find, but at least I'll feel like I'm doing something."

"We have internet here. You don't have to go off to

London."

She let him down gently: "I appreciate it, but I need a change of scenery. Walking around the city will help me think. Thank you for all your help today."

She stood up and yawned again. "Dinner was great, but I'm exhausted. I think I'll have a hot shower and turn in early. See you in the morning."

She left Henry staring into the fire. Another time, if she were at a different place in her life, she might be tempted to start something with him. But now she had only one focus, to find out what had really happened to Lucy. And there was no way she believed Lucy was in fairyland.

The simplest explanation. She should accept Lucy was gone. But if there was another explanation, she was determined to find it.

Melinda enjoyed her breakfast at the fancy hotel. The drive back yesterday had taken her all day. Of course, part of that was because she got lost several times, and then there were the sheep. At least three different times she found them blocking the road and had to wait until they decided to move on. By the time she got to London and checked in to the hotel, Melinda had been so exhausted she fell asleep without bothering to change out of her clothes.

The next morning, after a long, hot shower and a hearty

breakfast, she was feeling more like herself again. Time for a plan.

Walking always helped Melinda come up with her best ideas. She was known for pacing around her office and then calling out an idea or five. There was so much to see in the city that it wouldn't matter which direction she chose. Walking down a cobblestone street, Melinda felt lost, untethered to the world. It was something about all the history here that made you feel you could turn a corner and find yourself in another time. Now she was being fanciful. All the tales Magnus and Angus had told her going to her head.

She made her way to Trafalgar Square, where she aimlessly meandered, exploring shops and stopping for lunch. Not noticing where she was going, Melinda found herself in front of the National Gallery. She wandered through the museum, stopping and looking at whatever caught her eye.

Afternoon tea was something she could get used to. Melinda made a note to start the practice at home. It would be a nice way to break up the day of her boring corporate job. Taking the time to have a cup of tea and a little snack would refresh her during the dreaded afternoon slump. She liked her job, it just wasn't something she loved, and every day from three to four she felt like taking a catnap.

As she turned down one of the corridors in the museum, Melinda found herself all alone in the gallery. She admired the paintings, stopping to read some of the plaques. She was ready to call it a day, but a small painting in the far corner caught her eye. Something about the bright colors among the darker colors on the wall.

As she leaned close to get a better look, the world dropped out from under her. Melinda placed a hand on the wall to steady herself. The room started spinning and black spots somersaulted over each other before her eyes.

"Miss, are you okay?"

She opened her eyes to see a kindly guard looking down at her. She was sitting on the floor.

"What happened?"

"I was doing my rounds and saw you go down right hard. You women today. You don't eat enough, always trying to be skinny."

He looked her up and down. "You look fine to me. Better get some food in you."

"I will. Thank you for your concern." She got up, made sure she wasn't going to pass out again, and put a hand on his shoulder. "Thank you for helping me. I'll sit here for a few minutes then find something to eat."

The guard looked doubtful. Melinda crossed her fingers behind her back. "Promise."

She waited until he was gone. Coast clear, she stood inches from the small painting. Well, small compared to some of the works taking up half the wall from floor to ceiling. The canvas looked about sixteen by twenty inches. The piece was untitled. The card next to it read, *Noble family, fourteenth century.*

The painting depicted a sexy man with long black hair and emerald eyes. There were five children of various ages.

Four boys and one baby. But it was the woman in the painting that caused Melinda to wonder if she was hallucinating.

The woman in the painting was Lucy. How was it possible her sister was the subject of a painting from the fourteenth century?

Chapter Five

Melinda uploaded the picture of the painting she'd taken at the museum. She felt vaguely guilty. But it was more important to find out what had happened to her sister and why Lucy was the subject of a painting created at least seven hundred years ago than it was to worry about the light from the flash affecting the painting.

She ordered room service, put the *Do not disturb* sign on the door, and went to work on her iPad. One thing she knew: she was good at research.

"Charlotte. I've been trying to reach you all night."

It was a couple of hours later in Romania, but Charlotte

was still up. Her baby sister was so different. Charlotte was content to roam the globe with nothing more than a backpack, while Melinda preferred to live in the same town all her life and always over-packed. She worried Charlotte would never come back and would instead drift aimlessly, listening for something only she could hear.

"It's late, Mellie. What's wrong?"

"So how do you think our sister came to be the model for a painting dated sometime in the fourteenth century?"

Melinda waited for Charlotte to digest the entire story. When she'd left the museum, Melinda spent every moment searching for any information about her sister. Scrolling through thousands and thousands of images, and all she'd come up with was a big, fat nothing.

Charlotte let out a half-sigh, half-grunt, and Melinda swore she could feel the coming lecture all the way across the distance. Guess tonight Charlotte was playing the big sister role.

"Listen, sis, you need to get out. Go sightseeing. You're turning into a hermit. It isn't healthy. Don't you think it's time to accept Lucy's gone? She died. She didn't vanish. You've got to let go. Move on with your life."

"Is that what you're doing? Moving on with your life? It seems to me like you're running away. I don't want to argue. Didn't you hear me, other people have gone missing—"

"Stop. You're completely obsessed. You're only twenty-six, way too young to be so obsessed with death. Lucy has taken the next step in the journey."

"Don't give me that New Age hocus-pocus stuff. That's

what people say to make themselves feel better. I feel like there's a hole in my heart. I've tried, honestly. I don't know why I can't let this go." Melinda took a deep breath.

"Come to London. Are you still on the dig? Help me see what we can find. Together. There has to be an explanation."

"We're still in the Carpathian Mountains and we're snowed in. In fact, I'm surprised I can even get a cell signal. I'll always love Lucy, but I'm not going to shut my life down. She wouldn't want that. She'd want us to laugh and find someone to love and to go on living."

Melinda could hear Charlotte speaking to someone in the background, and then she came back on the phone.

"You know there is another explanation...they say everyone has a twin. I think you found Lucy's. Who knows; maybe the woman hanging on the wall is some old ancestor of ours."

Melinda had to agree. Her baby sister had a point. The explanation made sense, but it wasn't very satisfying. Was she looking too hard? Trying to find answers that weren't there?

"I booked my ticket for two weeks. I'm gonna stay, spend the rest of the time looking, and if I don't find anything then I'll come home. I'll say goodbye for good. Is that what you want to hear?"

Charlotte's voice was gentle across the miles. "I know it's hard. She'll always be our sister. We'll always love her. But it isn't healthy to obsess. Finish doing whatever you have to and get the feeling that she's still alive out of your system.

I'm not trying to be cruel, Mellie, just realistic. You know how you get. Call me when you get back home. How about this? I'll come home in time for Easter. We can make chocolate bunnies and dye eggs like when we were kids."

Melinda looked at the time on the phone. As late as it was, she might as well stay up. She scoured the internet looking for anything related to missing persons around Blackford Castle. Then she searched on time travel. Wow, so many search results. She found all kinds of way-out-there theories. Tons of fiction. Lots of romance books, some of which she noted to read for fun later, and way too much speculation. Not to mention all the occult books. They looked the most promising. Talk about some crazy ideas.

Melinda ordered an early breakfast from room service and ate in the room. She'd located a couple of bookstores nearby that offered a large selection of books on the occult.

The smell of incense in The Cauldron bookstore almost knocked her over. The proprietor acted like he was a wizard or some other magical being. She barely resisted the urge to laugh every time he popped up around the corner and peered at her through electric-blue glasses with pale blue lenses.

The shop was full of books on spells and New Age practices. Melinda swore she went through every book in the place. The only thing she seemed to find in common was they all thought certain days of the year were most favorable. Was it coincidence Lucy was lost on the first day of summer? It was one of the dates mentioned.

Could her sister somehow have gone back in time? And if

she did, how did she go back?

If these books had any truth to them, she was trying during the wrong time of year. Tomorrow was Valentine's Day. According to the books, the next favorable day would be the first day of spring, in late March. She didn't have that long to wait.

Three of the books had the most information. She felt a little silly believing in this hocus-pocus stuff, but if it worked...

When she leaned over to pick up her tote bag, her necklace fell out of her sweater.

The wannabe wizard reached for it. Melinda stepped back, not wanting him to touch it.

"Let me see?"

She held it up. "Look, don't touch."

He peered at the gems and charm on the heavy gold chain. "That necklace has power."

She forced herself not to roll her eyes, and instead plastered on her best fake smile. "So I've been told. What do I owe you?"

As she left the store, Melinda tucked the necklace under her shirt. She passed an advertisement for Stonehenge. It kept coming up. Like when you bought a certain kind of car and all of a sudden saw loads of them on the road.

Stonehenge. During her research, boatloads of mentions about Stonehenge kept popping up. People ascribed all kinds of supernatural happenings to the stones. It was worth a look.

There was one ticket left on a day trip by bus from

London to Stonehenge. Thank goodness for online booking. What did people do before the internet?

Melinda locked everything of value, including her passport, in the safe in her hotel. All she brought along was the room key, lip gloss, and money. She finished putting on all of her outerwear, then headed out of the hotel to meet the bus.

There was a seat in front by the window as she boarded the bus. Melinda settled in, took out her notebook and one of the new books, and started reading.

There were all kinds of people on the bus. Everyone from older couples and kids traveling for their gap years, to all the New Age hippies and self-described witches and warlocks. Many of them looked at her curiously or tried to engage her in conversation, but she shut them all down. She wasn't in the mood to talk or make friends. She was on a mission.

When they arrived, Melinda followed two girls with rainbow hair off the bus and into the cold wind. She could see the appeal of the place. There was some kind of energy in the air. Feelings of hope. Melinda walked around people-watching as she whispered over and over, "Take me to Lucy, take me to Lucy, take me to Lucy." She felt a little silly, but since no one could hear her, what could it hurt?

Several hours went by and it was time to board the bus back to London. Nothing had happened. No matter how hard she wished, no matter how many rocks she touched, she was still here. Maybe the woman was an ancestor. It certainly made more sense than believing her sister could've somehow traveled back in time.

But the idea wouldn't leave her head. And she wondered if you could go back, how could you control *when* you went back? Because even if she found a way, how would she know she had the right time period? All she knew was Lucy, or the woman who looked like Lucy, was in the fourteenth century. What if she got there at the beginning and Lucy didn't go back until the end? Or what if she got there at the end and her sister had died an old woman? Worse yet, what if she got there and Lucy wouldn't arrive for thirty years? Talk about a long wait.

Heck, what if she ended up in ancient Rome, Regency England, or, heaven forbid, what if she went all the way back to the time of the dinosaurs? Melinda certainly didn't relish becoming a lion or dinosaur snack.

By the time she arrived back at the hotel and enjoyed a nice, quiet dinner, she decided to go back to Blackford Castle one last time. She would search the grounds and outbuildings once more and then go home.

Melinda felt a little more comfortable driving on the left side of the road, though her sense of direction was abysmal. When she'd gone downstairs for breakfast, the hotel delivered flowers to her room. The card read, *Happy Valentine's Day. Miss you, sis. Love, Charlotte.* The bouquet was an assortment of flowers all in pink, white, and red. It was beautiful.

Lunch was fish and chips from a shop in a tiny town. Melinda thought she was on the right track in her journey, but later on, the signs looked wrong. Somehow she must've turned left when she should've turned right.

Instead of a sign for York, she saw a sign for Blackpool. She recognized the name from her map. "Crap on toast. I'm on the opposite coast."

A very unladylike word left her mouth as she looked for a place to turn around. Up ahead she saw a side road, turned right, and followed it. It was a narrow one-lane road with deep ditches on either side. She was afraid she'd get stuck if she tried to turn the little car around in the middle of the road, so she drove on looking for a wider place to turn around, hoping she wouldn't dead-end at the ocean. She could smell the sea. One of her favorite scents of all time.

Melinda came around a bend in the road. "What are the odds?"

A partially ruined castle stood on the rise, looking very forbidding and a little sad. It seemed to be abandoned. She didn't see any National Trust signs or car park areas with a ticket booth, so she found a grassy, flat area and parked.

Leave it to her to want to go to Blackford Castle and end up—where? It was a Merriweather family gift to be so awful with directions. Thunder boomed, and Melinda took note of the sky and the dark clouds. Looked like it would start storming any minute. She didn't want to be in the car in a middle of a field during a storm. Not since the accident she'd had in high school when she parked in a field, only to have the car sink up to the roof in mud during a thunderstorm.

Nope. The castle was a better choice. She grabbed her thermos and map and ran for the gate with the big, sharp teeth hanging down. Right, the portcullis.

It was cold with the wind blowing, but at least she was dry. That didn't last long. The rain started to blow sideways, and she would be soaked if she didn't move. The front door stood partially open.

She ran for it. "Don't let me get hit by lightning."

The door was heavy. She pushed but it wouldn't budge. Annoyed, she turned sideways, sucked in a deep breath, and tried to squeeze through. No go. She tried again and failed.

"Third time's the charm, right?" Melinda unbuttoned her coat, forced all the air in her lungs out, sucked in her tummy, and squeezed through, scraping her cheek as the storm started to howl.

The cavernous room smelled of the ocean, damp, and dust. That smell when a house sits empty and unloved for a long time. Dim afternoon light filtered in through holes in the wall. She looked up. Good. The roof was mostly intact.

Lightning made her jump, but illuminated a corner that might provide a better windbreak. Melinda walked past a fireplace large enough to have a party in and stopped to admire the carvings. There were falcons carved into the stone. This place must have been beautiful in its heyday. Why would anyone leave? This was security. If it were hers, she would never leave. Melinda blew on her hands to warm them. Completely preoccupied with her trip, she'd left the mittens behind at the chip shop.

As she made her way to the far corner, she spied some kind of wooden bench. Grateful she wouldn't have to sit on the cold stone floor, Melinda sat down and leaned against the wall.

Surely the storm would be over soon. She opened the map and used the light from her phone to illuminate the page.

Wow. Talk about a wrong turn. She was on the west coast of England instead of the east. She found the town of Blackpool and saw the Irish Sea. Blackford Castle was too far away to make the drive tonight. Being so unfamiliar with the small roads, she wasn't comfortable driving after dark. She'd have to find a place to stay and head to Blackford in the morning. Her cheek felt wet. She touched a finger to her skin. Blood. She must've really scraped her cheek.

The smell of ozone filled the air when the lightning struck, making her jump. It seemed awfully close. In the flash, she spied something in the rubble to her left.

Melinda knelt down on the floor where she saw the glint. There was a small object. If she could just reach it...

A shock jolted through her as her fist closed around the small, round object.

Chapter Six

February 1327—England

James Rivers, otherwise known as the Red Knight, blew the errant hair out of his eyes and surveyed the surroundings.

"Lord Falconburg, welcome to my humble keep."

Lord Rudley trembled at the sight of James and his men. He smiled on the inside. Truth be told, he liked the effect he had on men. His disfigurement made him even more fearsome.

James nodded at the man as he dismounted and tossed the reins to a waiting boy. The boy seemed transfixed by his face. James winked at him, and the child smiled. At least one small child wasn't afraid of him. The rest seemed to run and shriek whenever they caught sight of him.

His warriors made themselves comfortable. They would leave in the morning if all went well, adding a few more to their company.

He followed the man inside the keep, noting the faded tapestries and threadbare rugs. No wonder the man was so eager to wed his daughter to the renowned Red Knight. He was in sore need of gold.

A serving girl took one look at his face, shrieked, and dropped the tray of wine. The cup shattered and wine ran across the floor like blood on a battlefield.

"She's a nervous one, my lord." Lord Rudley twisted his hands and looked as if he were about to start weeping.

Other servants crossed themselves, young girls shrieked and ran from the hall, while several small boys seemed to be growing. James looked over his shoulder and counted five. As most boys, they were fascinated by scars. He knew if he bellowed they would jump in fright. He yawned, anxious to be on his way.

An older woman, one not easily scared, brought wine. She poured and left without uttering a word.

"I will depart in the morning. Will Eleanor be ready to travel?"

The man stammered and stuttered. "She will want to take her lady's maid along."

"I expected as much. Most ladies seem to travel with a great deal of belongings. My men will ensure she is well guarded."

A commotion sounded from the direction of the kitchens. James heard shrieking and the sound of breaking pottery. The girl in question came running into the solar.

"Father, I will not wed the beast. I would rather die." The

girl skidded to a stop as she caught sight of him sitting in a chair by the fire. Her mouth opened and closed several times, her eyes grew round, she made a strangled sound in her throat, and then she fainted in a small heap in the center of the room.

With his injured leg, James couldn't catch her in time. He cursed under his breath as her head banged against the stone floor.

Her father looked disgusted. "She is high-strung, nothing more. The priest is waiting."

More likely she was terrified of him, but the amount of gold James had offered ensured her father would give her to him. James snorted. For the amount of gold he was offering, her father likely wouldn't care what James did with the wench once he left the keep. He could only imagine the rumors about the unwholesome goings-on at Falconburg.

The girl's maid helped her up. Eleanor blinked several times. "Was I dreaming? Did the beast carry me away to his dark lair?" She trembled as a small mouse or rabbit caught in the gaze of a hungry falcon.

Then she looked at him. Stared at the scars on his face. James knew what was coming and put his fingers to his ears.

She let out a piercing shriek, jumped up, and fled her father's hall.

"No! I will not marry the beast. I cannot bear to look upon him. He will torture me. I would rather die."

Lord Rudley looked sheepish. "She will wed you, my lord. I will beat her until she says aye."

James wouldn't allow the girl to take a beating.

"She is young. I will not live with a wife who screams and faints every time she sees me." James stood. "Makes it rather difficult to produce an heir."

Lord Rudley pleaded, "Do not go. In time she will come to accept you. There is no need to break the betrothal."

James knew Eleanor would never look on him with anything other than revulsion. "I believe the betrothal is broken."

He made his way out of the keep, averting his eyes from each person he encountered so he wouldn't have to see the look of horror on their faces. 'Twas a new experience for a woman to scream in terror when she saw him. James was used to women throwing themselves at him. He was in a foul mood. He wanted children, needed an heir.

Mayhap he could find a wife who liked living in the dark. Or a blind wife. He called for the horses.

James slapped his captain on the back. "Eleanor finds me objectionable. There will be no nuptials."

Wisely, his captain remained mute.

James touched a hand to the long scars running down the right side of his aching face. 'Twas fortunate he had not lost the eye.

Now no fair lady in the realm would wed the beast of

Falconburg. The name bestowed by a nameless serving wench while he lay burning with fever in some cursed inn. The cheek. Court news took ages to travel the lands, but a name? James swore viciously under his breath. Seemed every lady of breeding knew it well.

He used to be considered handsome. Women flocked to his bedchamber. Now, no woman would plight her troth to him, not even for the considerable amount of gold he possessed. Once again he touched the wicked-looking scar as if it were a talisman with unnatural powers. Another scar started at the corner of his nose and ran down through the outer edge of his mouth to march across his chin and down his neck.

Not long after he and his battled-hardened warriors left the keep, they were surrounded by ruffians. James had wanted to avoid the forest, but knowing it was the faster way home, he'd ignored the warning in his gut.

Men dropped out of the trees without making a sound. He admired the skill. Though not the blade presently pointed at his throat.

"What have we here?"

James spoke in a quiet voice. "I am the Red Knight. Take your men and leave and I won't put you and your men to the sword."

A few of the ruffians laughed, while others talked amongst themselves, worried looks crossing their faces. He knew his reputation. He was only surprised their leader had not heard of him. His fame had spread since his last battle and subsequent scars.

Women might fear him, while men stood in awe of his scarred countenance. Some flinched and tried to hide the reaction. A hideous warrior made the minstrels swoon as they composed ballads to his fearsome reputation. If only they could conjure him a wife. Now he was destined to spend the rest of his days alone. A hermit in his castle. The rumors of unsavory doings would soon follow.

Out of the corner of his eye, James saw one of the men nock an arrow. Without thinking, he unsheathed the tools of his trade. 'Twas what he was known for, fighting with two swords. The name, the Red Knight, came from his blood-soaked armor and sword during battle. Even in the aftermath, his skin would be stained red for days from all the blood.

The skirmish was brief. He cut down the first with one thrust. And ran three more through while the men finished off the rest. Disgusted, James looked down at the motley group of men. Many of them looked hungry. They'd obviously been living in the forest, preying on unwary travelers. They chose the wrong men to trifle with this day.

Tired, his shoulder aching from the arrow wound, James shifted in the saddle. He wore silk under his tunic, as arrows could not pierce silk. The tip went in, taking the silk with it, and could be pulled out without leaving any fragments behind, thereby decreasing the chance the wound would putrefy.

He was distracted thinking of the look of horror on the girl's face when she had looked upon his visage, and it had cost him. 'Twas disappointing, to say the least. He frowned at the wound.

"You'll find another," his captain said.

James didn't pretend not to understand. They'd spent the past fortnight traveling throughout the realm searching for a bride. It seemed even a castle full of gold wasn't enough to entice a woman to spend the rest of her life gazing upon his ruined face.

He was the last of his name. James wanted a large family. Sons to carry on when he was gone. A woman to love. Now he would have none of those things.

Almost home, he urged the horse forward.

Chapter Seven

Melinda wiped greenish-black mud off the object. A gold ring lay in her palm, a big, fat sapphire winking up at her. With the hem of her coat, she rubbed the band. It was engraved with flowers, the work delicate. There was a nick halfway through the band, as if something sharp had sliced into it.

Outside, the storm raged, the sea crashing against the rocks, sending salty spray into the broken wall. It seemed no matter where she sat, Melinda was destined to be soaking wet by the time she left.

Something about the ring captivated. She slipped it on, watching it spin around. Too big. She tried the ring on her thumb.

"Ouch."

She pulled the ring off and looked at the drop of blood welling up on the inside of her thumb where the ring had cut her. She pulled out a tissue from the pocket of her coat and wrapped it around the jagged edge of the ring. Melinda couldn't say why, only that she needed to keep the ring close. She slid it back on her thumb, feeling the blood soak through the tissue, warm against her skin. The scent of copper filled the air, mingling with the salt spray.

Lightning struck so close she saw flashes of the pattern when she blinked. Her hair stood straight out. Her whole body felt like static electricity, alive and sparking. Random thoughts skittered around her head. How she must look like Medusa, with the corkscrew curls standing out all over her head instead of snakes.

A terrible sound of tearing metal filled the air. It was similar to when she'd been waiting at an intersection and two big trucks collided. An entire side of one of the trucks completely shorn off. Talk about a horrible screeching sound. It made her teeth ache long after the accident was over. Flashes of light filled her vision and she heard what sounded like voices.

"Who's there?"

She felt numb, as if she'd been outside in the snow for a very long time. The sounds and lights grew brighter, louder, and she shut her eyes, wishing they would go away. A sensation of being pulled under, like the undertow sweeping her beneath the waves, filled her. Melinda struggled, to no avail.

It was so quiet. Why couldn't she hear the ocean beating against the rocks? Melinda opened her eyes and sat up, brushing snow out of her hair. Wait. There was snow on the ground?

She turned her head from side to side. She was no longer inside the ruined castle. In fact, she couldn't even see the castle. She stood up, wobbled, then stretched her hands out wide to regain her balance. After a deep breath, she turned in a slow circle. Where was the road she'd driven in on? Not only that, where was the car? The castle? What on earth was going on?

A wave of dizziness crashed over her, and Melinda sat down before she fell over. A raven cawed, landing beside her in the snow, the black feathers stark against the white. He looked at her, cocking his head.

"Want to tell me where I am?"

Lovely. She must've hit her head when she fell to be having a conversation with a bird. The bird cocked his head again, cawed, and took to the air. Okay, maybe she wasn't the best company. She shivered. Melinda looked around for her coat but didn't see it. She remembered using the warm garment as a blanket when the storm hit. She'd wrapped it around her to keep warm. Great, no money either. It was in the pocket of her coat. Teeth chattering in the bitter cold, she stood and started walking. The fluffy snowflakes looked beautiful. They didn't get much snow in Holden Beach. In the distance she thought she heard the ocean, but which direction was it coming from?

Maybe she'd rolled down the hill when she fell? Melinda turned and began walking in what she thought was the direction she'd driven. Grateful she'd worn warm clothes and tall boots, she pulled her hands into the sleeves of the oversized sweater and stopped. Melinda looked at her left hand. Where was the ring?

The beautiful ring. Given its size, she knew it belonged to a man. Melinda didn't care for jewelry on men, though she could imagine this ring on a strong hand, its owner rugged and tall. She ran a finger over her thumb, felt the small cut, and knew she hadn't imagined the ring. Melinda looked around, thinking the ring would stand out in the snow, but didn't see it. It was too cold to spend the day looking. She'd freeze to death.

As she walked, she swore the landscape looked different. More wild and untamed. Melinda didn't know how long she walked, but certainly long enough that she should have found the road. Seen another car. At least moving kept her warm. Maybe she should change direction? While she stood still trying to decide which way to go, she heard thunder again. But different. Not a storm.

Men on horseback rode straight for her. And it looked like they were in a hurry. She squinted, because something looked out of place, but she couldn't quite put a finger on it. As they came closer, she could see what bothered her. The men were dressed in some kind of leggings, long shirts, and long cloaks. And were those swords? She blinked three times. Yep, swords.

Her heart beat in double time as the big question flashed in neon lights. Had she done it? Really gone back in time? The rest of her thoughts were cut short as one of the men unsheathed his sword and swung at her head.

Common sense, or fear, or whatever you wanted to call it, kicked in at the last moment, and Melinda dropped to all fours. When she could breathe again, she stood to give them a piece of her mind. Five men surrounded her.

A kind of shaky feeling in her stomach telling her something was wrong wiggled around her gut and made her bones feel like they'd turned to jelly. She wobbled but didn't fall. The men looked like the kind of guys any rational woman would cross the street to avoid. Not only did they look mean, they looked dangerous.

The man who'd swung at her dismounted from his horse, came to stand in front of her, and started yelling. She listened but couldn't make out what he was saying. It kinda sounded like French, but she didn't speak French, so she wasn't really sure. She'd been to Paris once, but this sounded different. Maybe another region in France? Crap on toast, had she gone back in time only to end up in France instead of England?

As she was trying to figure out where she was and when she was, the man grabbed hold of her.

"Take your hands off me now or lose them." She glared back at the man. Mean men were like mean dogs: never show fear.

By this time the other men had dismounted and surrounded her. She had a bad feeling. But she would brazen it out. She turned and looked each one of them in the eye, giving them her meanest look.

"My boyfriend will be along shortly. You better not touch me."

It seemed the wrong thing to say. The men grabbed at her hair and took hold of her arms. Blackness rose deep within. She felt hot all over. There was no one around. No one to save her if these men decided to hurt her. Or do something much worse. She kicked the man closest to her as hard as she could. Using the palm of her hand, she pushed another one hard enough to make him fall over backward. She felt hair tearing from her scalp as she turned and ran.

Up ahead she could see trees. If she could make it into the woods, maybe she could hide. Melinda ran for all she was worth. She heard cursing behind her, knew if they got on their horses they'd capture her in a minute. The sounds of men yelling to each other filled the air. It sounded like they were getting back on their horses. Behind her, she heard heavy breathing. Risking a quick look over her shoulder, Melinda let out a yelp. The man was so close he could almost grab her. Fear gave her speed. Thank the stars she'd worn practical low-heeled boots instead of heels. She ran as fast as she could, panting and sweating. She hadn't even run this fast at last year's Lilly Pulitzer sample sale.

The trees were so close. Yes. She was going to make it. And as that tiny flicker of hope blossomed inside, the heavy breather tackled her from behind. She went down, the breath knocked out of her. Melinda struggled to pull air into her lungs and knew how fish must feel when they're caught and thrown on the dock.

He straddled her, leaned close to her face, leering. She gagged from the smell of his breath. He was missing several teeth, and the rest of them looked awfully yellow. Didn't they brush their teeth here? Oh, my. He smelled like he slept in garbage. She gagged. Yuck.

"Get off me." Melinda thrashed, bucking to dislodge him, but the man seemed glued to her. Smelly Breath pulled a piece of dirty cloth from somewhere on his person and tied it around her mouth. She dry-heaved against the cloth, trying not to throw up. The scrap of fabric smelled awful. And the taste—she didn't want to think about where it had been or what she was tasting. Double yuck.

The rest of the men caught up to them. And the one she'd kicked in the family jewels returned the favor, kicking her in the side and sending her to her knees. Hard enough she saw spots in front of her eyes. She swallowed down the nausea and bit the inside of her cheek hard enough to draw blood. *You can't pass out. If you do, they'll rape you.*

The man she'd pushed held the other one back. He rubbed his clavicle and spat. The glob of icky yellow stuff landed next to her knee and a fresh wave of nausea rolled over her.

"I get first go."

Another of the men peered dubiously at her. "Are you sure 'tis a woman? She's unnaturally tall. Mayhap 'tis a pretty boy."

Smelly Breath grabbed her.

"She's a woman." He leered to his friends as he untied the gag and kissed her.

Gross. He slobbered all over her face as she pushed him away. He laughed. Melinda spat at him even as a voice in the back of her head told her it was completely unladylike and she should be ashamed. It was the perfectly proper voice of Aunt Pittypat, who was a hippie with flawless manners. She'd dance naked under a full moon and serve snacks afterward on china that was two hundred years old.

Some of the men lost interest. Now only two men surrounded her. The leader and the one she'd kicked. The rest seemed to be taking care of the horses and other camping-type stuff. She hated to camp.

Melinda tried to scream, but with the gag back in place, all she managed to do was make herself feel like she was going to barf any second. Somehow she managed to stand and wipe her face off on her shoulder. It was hard to breathe through her nose. It felt hot and swollen. There was dried blood crusted in the corner of her mouth. She could taste it over the foul gag.

"A saucy wench. Move aside and give me a taste." The man she'd kicked pulled her down on the ground, removed the gag, and proceeded to inhale her face.

Stupid. Hadn't he learned from his friend? Melinda bit his cheek. He howled in pain and slapped her across the face. Little unicorns and birds flew around in circles. Ice coated her insides. She managed to roll out from under him. Before she could stand and run, something cold pressed against her stinging cheek.

"Run and I will cut your pretty face from ear to ear."

She froze on her hands and knees as if she were moving into a yoga pose. Very slowly she eased back on her heels, the knife never leaving her face. The tip of the blade pressing into her cheek. Melinda used to complain men saw her face first and never cared about her mind. She'd grumped to her friends how some days she wished she weren't pretty.

Sorry, universe. I swear I didn't mean it. I like my face. Please don't let them hurt me.

Sweetness might work. It couldn't hurt. "What are y'all doing out here? If you'd remove the sword, I would feel a whole lot better."

The man cocked his head, spoke to the leader in that odd French, then sneered at her.

"You are alone, demoiselle. You come with us." He moved the blade while the other one tied her hands in front of her, then tied her feet.

Thank goodness he didn't notice she'd kicked the gag away. Great, just freaking great. Melinda filled her stomach with breath and pushed it out as far as she could, hoping it might give a tiny bit of slack as the man tied her to the tree.

The leader sneered at her. "Pleasure us well and we may let you live."

She gulped. Not gonna happen. Melinda opened her mouth and let out her best horror-movie scream.

"Scream for me again, wench. Allow me the joy of cutting out your pretty green eye and sucking out the juices."

Ick. How disgusting. She shut her mouth with a snap. *This is what you get for making plans. Betcha didn't plan on being kidnapped and ravaged by a group of horrible men.* The voice in her head sounded so smug and self-righteous. This wouldn't do. She had to get away and find out where and when she was.

While her captors ate lunch, she tested the ropes. There was a bit of slack around her, and she leaned back and forth, trying to stretch the rope. When one of the men looked her way, she pretended to be fascinated with the trees around her. He went back to eating and she worked on the knots around her wrists. There was no way she would be the dessert.

Chapter Eight

"Halt." James swore he heard a woman scream. The feminine sound of distress carried across the wood. He'd seen enough of the horror women faced during battle. He would allow no harm to come to those on his land.

James urged the horse onward and into the wood to render aid. A young boy—no, 'twas a girl—ran through the woods, a look of fear upon her face. Five men chased her. Bandits from lands to the south, trying to steal from him again. This winter was not as severe as the past few; the terrible famine was now over and food was more plentiful. However, some men, once turned thief, found the taste as filling as a cup of ale and would not turn back.

The witless female stopped and stood in the grass, gaping at him, mouth open, about to find her head separated from her shoulders.

He urged the horse to a gallop, metal screeching against metal as he unsheathed his sword, met the bandit's blade, and saved the wench. The clang of swords rent the air as his men dispatched the ruffians. 'Twas over before James began to sweat. He leaned negligently against a tree, longing for one good fight.

Where was the feebleminded lass? He heard the sound of a wounded animal coming from the trees. James tied the horse to a tree. He moved through the woods and found her on the ground, curled up into a small ball. As if she could disappear if she made herself small enough. She sat in the snow, head in her hands, muttering strange words.

He knelt down beside her, grunting at the ache in his leg. James raised a hand to pat her shoulder, then stopped. He did not know how to soothe her tender feelings, so he clapped her on the shoulder.

"How do you fare?"

He cast a baleful eye over her while she babbled. Something gleamed like burnished metal in the weak afternoon sun. James reached down and picked up a lock of hair. She'd almost lost her pretty head.

The hair was glorious. Shades of copper, the red of a sunset, and the dark wine color of dried blood, which, oddly enough, he found quite beautiful. The coil wrapped around his finger, and when he pulled it out, the curl sprang back, curling around his finger as if it did not want to let go. Without thinking, he tucked the lock into a pouch at his waist.

James leaned close, gentling his voice. "My lady, are you injured?"

She spread her fingers, peeking through them, but did

not answer. He spoke to her again, the pain in his legs threatening to topple him over as he crouched beside her. James prayed he would be able to stand without falling over and making a fool of himself.

She removed her hands from her face. Brilliant green eyes stared up at him.

"I can't really understand you. Are you speaking French?"

She was speaking a form of English, though her speech sounded odd, the accent strange yet soothing. Soft. Caressing him like a lover.

"I inquired if you were injured, lady."

She held up her hands and he could see the ropes binding them. With one swipe of his blade, the rope fell to the ground. He took her hands in his, anger filling him upon noting the angry red marks encircling her slim wrists. She had beautiful skin. Unmarked and unblemished, as fine as ivory. Realizing he was stroking circles on her wrist, he dropped her hands as if they were on fire.

"I don't think..." She touched a hand to her cheek. "He nicked me, but it's only a scratch. My nose hurts like crazy."

James touched a finger to her cheek where the blade had left its mark. It was only a scratch, and she would heal. The nose was swollen but looked straight. He'd suffered many a broken nose, enough to know she was fine. There was dried blood above her lip. He wiped at it with his thumb, touching her lip. The skin was soft as a rose petal.

"'Tis fortunate you did not lose your head, lady."

"I am rather attached to it." She smiled at him. He felt

strange inside, as if he'd been inside all winter locked in the dark and just stepped out into the light, blinking and marveling at the colors around him.

As he was wondering how he was going to manage to stand, his captain appeared by his side, sensing his distress. Renly helped them both up while making it look as if he wasn't holding James up.

"Thank you for rescuing me. They were going to... Well, it doesn't matter now that I'm safe." She wrapped her arms around herself and, realizing she was freezing, James unclasped his cloak and settled it around her shoulders.

She placed a hand on his forearm. Heat from her touch traveled up his arm straight to his battered heart.

"I was wondering, could you tell me what day it is?"

His captain answered, "'Tis the fourteenth of February, my lady."

"I hope you won't think it's weird, but could you also tell me the year?"

Renly gaped. James blinked. From her clothing, he surmised she was highborn, yet from her speech he wasn't sure, unless she hailed from a distant land. But to ask him the year—mayhap she'd hit her head during the encounter. He decided to humor her.

"'Tis the year of our Lord 1327."

"Oh. Um... Am I in France?"

How could she not know what country she was in? Was the girl witless? It would be his fate to meet such a fetching wench and have her be feeble. Perchance if she was, she might be the only wench in all the realm that would consider marrying a beast such as he. For she had not blubbered and run after looking upon his face. Certainly 'twas a good omen.

"Nay, lady. You are in England. On my lands. We are not far from Falconburg Castle."

She heaved a great sigh of relief.

"Oh good. I know Falconburg. I was there earlier today." Then she slapped a hand over her mouth, as if she shouldn't have said such a thing. And all manner of alarm swept through him. Had she been sent by one of his many enemies? Perchance sent to taunt and torture him.

She reached out a hand to touch his face, and he flinched.

"You're hurt. A cut." She touched a finger to his eyebrow and held it up. It came away red. He reached a hand up to his face.

"'Tis naught but a scratch. Nothing to worry yourself over, my lady." She would plague him. All women were afraid of him. He knew an enemy had sent her, for she showed no fear to get him to let down his guard. He must watch her and uncover whatever intrigue she was plotting.

"How did you come to be on my land, lady? Where is your escort?"

She was saved from answering when the falling snow turned to stinging sleet. The men were all mounted and ready to ride, except for his captain. Renly boosted the girl up onto James' horse. He cupped his hands. James nodded, grateful for aid. His leg burned from kneeling so long, his shoulder pained him, and his head ached.

He sat behind her with a groan. "You can tell me how you came to be on my lands unescorted and in the clutches of bandits when we reach Falconburg. You need a warm drink and a bath."

She was shivering. James wrapped his cloak around them both, pulling her against his chest to let his body warm her. She stiffened for a moment then relaxed.

James knew they were merely a short distance from the castle, yet it seemed to take a fortnight to reach home. She reached out to touch his face without recoiling in horror. Every other lady in the realm ran screaming. Did she truly not care what he looked like? James was suspicious of this woman who did not fear him. Was not affronted by his visage.

Truth be told, she vexed him. The fact she seemed to find him not pleasing but perchance acceptable made James wary.

What was she doing at his home? Had the men they encountered been a ruse? She needed to be careful, for he had encountered those men before. They would have assaulted her then left her for dead or killed her when they'd slaked their needs.

The lady traveled with no companions. James and his men saw no sign of anyone else. He expected to find a carriage or a horse, perhaps belongings. Yet they found nothing. 'Twas as if she'd sprung up from the grass fully formed and ready to cause him trouble.

The wench in question had fallen asleep against his chest. She breathed in noisily through her swollen nose, sounding like one of his dogs. Her hair was soft like silk against his chin. She was tall for a woman, and shapely. He felt her curves as she leaned against him. Found himself staring at her legs. What kind of woman went about wearing men's hose? And her tunic. He had never seen such fine garments. He shifted in the saddle, trying to ease the pain in his hip, and by moving he woke her.

"Holy cow! Is that Falconburg?"

James was perplexed. She'd told him she came from his home earlier in the day, and yet her reaction bespoke of never seeing the castle before.

"Aye, lady."

She craned her head up to look at him. "It's quite breathtaking, isn't it? My name is Melinda. Melinda Merriweather."

He was filled with pride that she found his home pleasing. "I am James Rivers. Lord Falconburg. You may call me James."

"I can't believe I'm really here."

She seemed filled with joy at seeing his home. Being with him. And James was intrigued. He vowed to find out everything he could about Melinda Merriweather.

Chapter Nine

So far she'd lost the sapphire ring she'd found in the rubble, been abducted by a group of smelly men, knocked around a bit, and just when she thought she was going to die, *he'd* showed up.

Melinda had been so busy trying to escape that it took her a moment to process what was happening. The man, James, was unlike any man she'd ever seen back home. His thick black hair reached his shoulders and looked like it was long overdue for a trim. Yet it was his eyes that held her. They were a clear green that reminded her of the ocean. But on a man that would just be silly. And what a waste. She knew women who would kill for his eye color.

Melinda wasn't sure if her body shaking was from the cold or the adrenaline wearing off. She'd never experienced anything of the sort before. The closest she'd come to violence had been when some teenage boy stole her parking spot during a downpour, making her ruin her favorite heels.

Maybe coming to the past wasn't the best idea. She frowned. No matter. Even with everything so far, she'd do it again if it meant finding Lucy.

She'd really done it. Gone back in time. Melinda made a face. She thought knights were supposed to be chivalrous. James hadn't even helped her up on the horse; he just stood there watching her with a weird look on his face. She felt like an incompetent child as she tried to climb into the saddle. *Come on, it's not like everyone goes around riding horses every day. I'd like to see you drive a car.* Barely, just barely, she managed to resist sticking her tongue out at her savior. Not very grateful behavior, but then again, he made her feel like a child scolded for coloring outside the lines. When that man, Renly, had helped her up, she wanted to hug him.

The good captain had also helped James up on the horse. She scooted forward to give him space. He was huge. They both just fit on the horse. Melinda kept looking at the ground. It seemed a lot further to fall from way up here. In reality, she knew there was plenty of room on the horse. It was more the feeling of him behind her, his thighs pressing against hers. Riding together was intimate.

Maybe he was some kind of spoiled entitled nobility? Though he didn't seem jerky.

"Oh my gosh! It's not a ruin."

As they approached the castle, Melinda heard the voice of Aunt Pittypat in her head. *Better shut your mouth before you swallow a bug, sugar.*

James looked down at her, a questioning look on his

face. She didn't bother to answer. She was too busy looking at everything around her. She could hear the ocean pounding against the rocky shoreline. And as they approached the castle, she could see small freshwater lakes. A fish jumped, breaking the reflection.

"Are those saltwater or freshwater?"

He looked to where she was pointing. "The meres are freshwater, fed from a spring. They are stocked with fish to supply the kitchens."

She could see the main gates reflected in the water. The castle dominated the landscape. It was all very medieval and forbidding. Good luck to the enemy trying to breach these walls. Talk about awe-inspiring.

As they rode through the portcullis, she looked up at the spikes. It was a strange feeling, knowing she'd looked at the same spikes in her own time, where the castle and outbuilding were ruins. Now everything looked...not new, but lived in. The whole scene was nothing like she expected. Where were the starving, smelly people and half-rotten vegetables? A small half-laugh, half-sob escaped. Everything she knew about medieval life was gleaned from books, movies, and television. Would it be enough to help her navigate through the times?

The map she'd looked at when she sheltered from the storm showed Blackpool. Falconburg Castle wasn't far from the village. And Blackpool was about two hundred and fifty miles from the Scottish border. She kept trying to orient herself for when she could set out and look for Lucy. Know which way to go.

Hopefully this man would help her. If he wouldn't go with her, at least he might lend her a horse and some supplies so she could find her sister. Blackford Castle, the last place Lucy was seen alive. If Lucy wasn't there, where on earth would she look? It wasn't like she could open up a web browser and search for Lucy Merriweather.

Melinda turned her head side to side so many times, taking in everything as they rode into the castle proper, that her neck ached. She had to give whoever had built the thing credit. By riding through those freshwater ponds and the Irish Sea on the other side, it basically turned the castle into an island with only one approach. Talk about intimidating your enemies.

Melinda wasn't sure how she went back in time, but however she did, she was ever so grateful. She sent up a word of thanks to whoever was listening.

"I don't mean to repeat myself, but what year did you say it was?"

He looked at her as if she were an annoying toddler before answering. "The year of our Lord 1327."

Elated, Melinda fist-pumped the air.

"By the saints, are you unwell?"

Maybe a bit too exuberant a reaction.

"I'm fine. Just happy to be here."

She'd really done it. If only she knew how. Did it have something to do with the storm? She wasn't sure. And then the more obvious question...could she get back to the future? Charlotte would be beside herself when she found out yet another sister had gone missing and was now presumed dead.

What would the authorities say? That she'd committed suicide—filled with grief over losing her sister, did herself in?

James' men dismounted. Instead of dismounting, he sat there waiting like some warrior king, and she wondered, what for? Was he one of those guys who had to be all Lord of the Manor?

"My lady?"

One of the men held out his hands, and Melinda let him help her off the horse. She was unstable for a moment after riding for so long, but found her balance and stood, stretching out the kinks. She turned in time to see the same man helping James off the horse.

And then she knew.

She should've guessed by the horrible scars on such an otherwise strong and handsome face. He'd obviously been injured recently. She could tell by how badly he was limping. She felt like a complete witch thinking such mean thoughts about him when he obviously couldn't help her. What kind of doctors did they have nowadays?

A plump older woman came bustling over and the courtyard erupted into chaos.

"What have we here?"

James finished speaking with his men and came over to the woman. "This is Melinda Merriweather. See she has a bath and something hot to eat."

Before Melinda had a chance to thank him, she was bustled inside. A bath would be heavenly. She didn't care if every person in the castle was put to work heating the water; she was dying to get warm.

"Come along, child. You may call me Mrs. Black."

"Melinda. Melinda Merriweather."

She followed the woman up several flights of stairs. The woman pushed open a heavy door. It was some kind of bedroom. She didn't have time to look around, as she was ushered into a small alcove off the room. It contained a large wooden tub with some kind of cloth padding. Smart. Then the user wouldn't get splinters in their hiney. Small boys filled pots from a pipe sticking out of the wall. They poured the water into a huge black cauldron over a hearth. The fire crackled, and she could feel the warmth thawing her bones.

As she waited for them to finish heating the water and filling the tub, she looked around the bedroom. She expected Spartan and cold, no color. But this. The room was colorful and smelled of herbs. The fabrics were sumptuous, with beautiful rugs scattered over the stone floor and a couple of tapestries on the whitewashed walls. No smelly straw or threadbare blankets. James obviously had money.

"Mistress? Your bath is ready." The woman sent the boys out and handed her what looked like a lump of soap, a square of linen, and a comb made out of bone.

"Thank you."

A young girl walked in balancing a tray of food and drink. Melinda sniffed. Wine and beef stew? Who cared what it was? She was ravenous.

"I don't want the water to get cold."

"Mrs. Black said eat a few bites and you'll feel better."

She sat at a small table and quickly ate the entire bowl. A hunk of bread made a great sponge to soak up what was left. Another glass of wine and she felt flexible enough to undress. A groan left her lips as she sank into the steaming water.

"Lady? I'm to take your garments to be laundered." The girl looked to be around ten. She stood there blushing and shuffling her feet.

"Thank you very much. And thank you for the food. I was really hungry."

The little girl gathered up the garments, admiring the stitching.

"On second thought, you better leave them. I don't have anything else to wear."

"I will inform Mrs. Black. She will procure you proper garments. While you bathe, I will clean the mud off and place the clothes by the fire to dry. You have pretty skin, mistress. And your hair."

The little girl pointed to Melinda's hair, which looked like a mess, all things considered.

"I've never seen such curly red hair before. 'Tis very pretty."

And with that, the little girl scampered out of the small room. Melinda could hear her singing softly to herself in the bedroom as she scrubbed the leggings and shirt. Hopefully she wouldn't shrink the sweater in the hot water. She took a sip of wine and dunked her head, scrubbing her scalp. It felt marvelous to sit and soak. She had to come up with a story of why she was here.

Melinda must've dozed off while she was in the tub. Guess she was more tired than she thought.

"Lady? I'm here to help ye." Another girl stood waiting. This one looked to be around twelve. She helped Melinda out of the tub, efficiently dried her off, and led her over to the fire to dress in the slightly damp but much cleaner clothes. They'd have to do until she had something else to wear. Until she did, she could wash them out each night before bed and hang them to dry by the fire.

"These are men's hose." The girl sounded scandalized.

Melinda closed her mouth to keep from laughing out loud. She didn't want to embarrass the girl.

"This is what ladies wear where I come from."

The girl looked dubious, but handed Melinda the leggings and watched as she slipped them on.

When she woke this morning, she'd been so excited to get going, she'd forgotten to put on undies. Probably for the best now. As to her bra? She needed it for now.

"What is this, lady?"

The girl held up the bra, peering at it closely.

"It's called a bra. Goes on like this."

She couldn't believe she was dressing in front of this kid. At the gym was one thing. Everyone went about their business and no one stared. But the girl looked over every inch of her. Melinda turned pink.

The girl wrinkled her nose.

"'Tis an odd garment."

Bras hadn't been invented yet, and by the reaction, Melinda didn't worry she'd done anything to change history. She pulled on the long-sleeved shirt and then the oversized sweater. The little girl kept touching the sweater, and when she picked up Melinda's boots, she stroked the leather.

"'Tis so soft."

"They were awfully muddy. Please thank whoever cleaned them off while I was bathing."

The little girl bobbed a curtsy and left the room. As she was leaving, the older woman, Mrs. Black, came bustling in. The woman was always in a hurry.

Mrs. Black eyed Melinda up and down.

"You are tall for a lady, mistress. Have no worries, I will find you something more fitting to wear." She clapped her hands together. "Lord Falconburg is hearing a dispute. Come along and we'll find you something more to eat."

"Thank you. I'm so hungry I could eat a horse."

The woman looked horrified, but shut her mouth and led Melinda to the kitchens. There a servant put another bowl of the hearty stew and a piece of thick bread in front of her.

Chapter Ten

Left to her own devices over the next week, Melinda explored the grounds. She didn't have a guard, but no matter where she went, there was always someone watching. So she was a guest but not someone trusted. If a stranger showed up in her backyard looking for help, Melinda would probably call the cops. It wasn't safe anymore to take in strangers. Maybe things hadn't changed as much as she thought. She waved at her pretend guard and went on her way.

"Lady?"

She turned and looked into green eyes with impossibly long and thick lashes.

"Lord Falconburg. It's a pretty day."

He looked to the sky. "Aye." James shifted from foot to foot. "Here. Buy yourself a ribbon for your hair." He handed her a few coins. "If it pleases you."

"Thank you. I lost my money...during my travels."

The man in front of her looked unconvinced but didn't say anything. It was true. Her money was in her coat pocket somewhere in the castle...over seven hundred years from now.

"The dress looks lovely."

She touched the soft wool. It was a heather gray and made her feel like she didn't stick out so much. There was a belt with a small pouch hanging from it. Melinda put the coins inside, once again wishing for pockets.

She thanked him.

"Walk with me?"

He took her hand, drawing it through the crook of his elbow, then stiffened, as if she wouldn't want to take his arm. And that was when she thought he must have been sexy and charming before the accident. Sure of himself. He was still sexy, and she could see charm buried underneath his frown. Now he seemed to hide behind the scars and a grumpy demeanor.

James started to pull away, but she pulled on his elbow. "I saw the blacksmith making something. Would you explain its purpose?"

He looked relieved and pulled her along. Aunt Pittypat was right. When in doubt, ask a man to talk about himself or explain something. Worked every time. Melinda trotted to keep up. It was weekly market day. It was fun to see so many people and explore the vendors and goods.

James didn't say much. She felt awful when they passed a couple of pretty teenage girls and they shrank back. He stiffened, and Melinda could almost see the black mood hovering above his head.

He bought her a few ribbons to tie back her hair. She exclaimed over the dried and candied fruit, and he bought her candied cherries.

"These are so good. Sure you don't want one?"

He didn't smile, but didn't look as cranky. "It pleases me to see you smile."

"Lord Falconburg?"

James turned to one of his knights. Melinda nibbled the cherries and eyed a merchant selling fabrics.

"I take my leave of you."

She watched him go. They hadn't discussed why she was here yet. From the looks of things, he was in constant demand. He'd get to her eventually. In the meantime, she hadn't found anyone that knew Lucy. The plan to go to Blackford was the best idea she had. Now to get up the courage to ask James for a horse and help getting there.

Melinda went inside to the kitchens to find the two girls who'd been assigned to help her. She wanted to give them the rest of the candied cherries. While she still didn't have a good feel for the cost of things, she gathered they were expensive because of the sugar. The girls would love them.

"Mistress Merriweather." The cook handed her a roll, hot from the oven. Melinda put a bit of butter on it and sat at the table to eat, enjoying the warmth after being outside.

She was almost finished when a man ambled in. Melinda knocked a bowl off the table, the pottage splattering across the floor. A dog darted in, licking up the mess. With a shaking finger, she pointed at the man's neck.

"Where did you get that?"

Chapter Eleven

Melinda chased the poor man out of the kitchen and into the courtyard. She had to weave in between the crowds to keep up with him. As he turned the corner, she reached out and snatched his cloak.

"I'm so sorry, but I have to know, where did you get the scarf?"

The man looked nervous. What? Did he think she'd strike him? She smiled and stepped back a pace. He visibly relaxed.

"From Lady Blackford. She made it for me after she saw me admiring a brightly colored scarf the stable master wore. She's been teaching others to make them. Now they're sold at the weekly market at the castle." He fingered the end of the scarf. "'Tis very warm."

"Wait. Blackford? As in Blackford Castle?"

The man nodded, grinning at her as he stroked the beautiful gray scarf. "Don't know of any other Lady

Blackford."

"Lady Blackford. When did you see her last?"

The man tapped his finger against his chin, thinking. His face brightened. "'Twas a few months ago, lady. Do you know the Lady of Blackford?"

Melinda thought she was going to pass out. Was Lucy actually here in 1327? She'd come back to the right time.

"What does the lady look like?"

The man didn't seem surprised by the question. Then again, it wasn't as if people traveled back and forth across the coast every day. Some of the castle folks had never left Falconburg lands.

"She's lovely. An older lady, mind. Beautiful silver hair. And lively blue eyes."

Melinda's heart sank. She didn't know when crochet had been invented, but seeing the scarf made her think Lucy was here. Now, hearing this man's description, she shook her head, it couldn't be right. Lucy had long brown hair. She wasn't gray. Melinda thought back to the museum. The woman in the painting. Her hair was up, but Melinda swore it was dark, not silver. The information was a good lead. One that begged investigating.

"One last question. How far is it to Blackford Castle?"

The man was interrupted when a young boy appeared. "I'm to take you to Lord Falconburg."

She waved at the man. "Thank you, and enjoy the scarf."

He smiled and went on his way.

The boy led her through twisting passageways. There was no way she'd find her way back to her room. They came to a heavy wood door.

The boy knocked and gestured for her to go in. She stood in some kind of study. Masculine and oh so dark inside. In the short time she'd been in the past, Melinda had grown used to the lack of electricity, but she expected a few candles to be lit.

"Leave the lady with me."

The boy nodded, shutting the door behind him. Not sure what to do, Melinda stood in the center of the room. Being in such a different time, she knew to be careful what she did and said. From what she'd seen, she accepted she was living in a violent time. Sure, the U.S. had its share of violence, but at least in the present she had some semblance of authority, and social media to document every moment of everyone's life.

Here, though—say the wrong thing and find your head rolling down a hill. The last thing she wanted was to find herself tied to a stake, the villagers bearing torches, ready to burn her for being a witch.

"Sit by the fire. Warm yourself. Did you enjoy the market?"

"Yes, thank you." She dug in the pouch at her waist.

She noted James stayed behind the huge desk in shadow and darkness. Seemed a bit silly. She'd already seen his face. Spent hours looking at it as they traveled from the woods to the castle and every day since. What had happened to him? The scars looked recent. Still not sure what kind of man she was dealing with, Melinda held off on asking about Blackford Castle.

"I didn't spend much." She set the coins on his desk.

He looked surprised. "Keep the coin."

Melinda put them back in the pouch. They'd come in handy when she was traveling across the coast.

"I didn't get a chance to thank you for rescuing me. And for the hospitality."

He inclined his head, or at least she thought he nodded. It was kind of hard to tell in the dim light.

"Sit by the fire. Why were you traveling without escort? What were you doing on my lands?"

Talk about a man of few words. Melinda wouldn't be snarky. She needed a place to stay until she could find Lucy and go back home.

"Are you a learned man, Lord Falconburg?"

She couldn't see his face in the darkness, but she could feel the curiosity from across the desk.

"I am educated, lady. Why do you ask?"

She stood up and came closer, intending to sit beside the desk, where she could see his face and gauge his reactions.

"That's close enough. Stay by the fire." He must have realized how rude he sounded, for he said, "You needs be warm. You are wet from the rain. I wouldn't want a fever to take you."

Melinda didn't play games. Never understood the whole playing hard to get thing. She decided the best tack was the truth. Even though it was going to make her sound crazier than her famous great-grammy Lucy Lou Merriweather.

"It's kind of a long story. Might we have something to drink?" Yep, stalling, but she needed a few more minutes to gather her nerve.

A soft groan was the only indication James moved. The rug muffled his footsteps. When she looked up, he stood in front of her, pouring the wine. The firelight cast half his face in shadow.

Before the scars, he must have been beautiful. While most women would call him ugly or beastly, Melinda found him incredibly attractive. The scars gave him depth, made one look past the pretty. Scars on this man told of someone who could take care of himself. A man who could take care of others.

Obviously realizing it was going to be futile to go back to his desk. James limped to the chair across from her and sat down with a groan. She pretended not to notice. His injuries seemed to bother him more as the day went on. By dinner he visibly limped.

"The reason I ask if you're educated is because my story is going to seem unbelievable." She drank half the wine and refilled the goblet. Telling the truth was harder than she thought. Since she couldn't come up with a plausible story for why she was traveling alone, and dressed strangely, Melinda decided the truth was the best bet.

For some reason she knew he would be able to sense if she were lying. Instinct told her if he thought she lied, he would refuse to help. Thus far he was the best bet for someone to help her. Given she needed all the help she could get navigating the strange and unfamiliar terrain, she would be upfront with him.

"The reason you found me alone is because I am alone. I

was looking for my sister and I got turned around and ended up at your castle. Only I didn't know was your castle. You see, when I was visiting your castle it was...a ruin."

She stopped and looked at him to gauge his reaction. He was leaning forward in the chair, elbows resting on his knees, hands clasped together under his chin. He watched her, and she felt like a schoolgirl sent to the principal's office for putting gum in Nosy Nellie's hair.

He bared his teeth. "My castle in ruins. Are you feebleminded?"

She couldn't help it—she laughed. Not a normal laugh, more like some kind of strange, hysterical half-laugh, half-sob.

"If only. But no, I'm fine. When I woke on the day you found me, it was February fourteenth...2016. And then you told me the year is 1327. That's why I'm alone and why your castle was a ruin."

She whispered, "I'm from the future."

Chapter Twelve

Did Melinda Merriweather think him daft? The future? James leaned back in the chair to ease the ache in his hip, watching her through narrowed eyes.

His curiosity seemed to rule him, for he opened his mouth and said, "Tell me exactly what happened."

It wasn't question, it was a command. He waited to hear what she would say. What nonsensical ravings she would speak.

"As I said, I'm from the future."

Melinda fidgeted in her chair. Was she going to lie to him? He could not abide liars. She opened her mouth, and he noticed her and straight white teeth.

"You see, my sister went missing. It was on the first day of summer. She'd come to England with her jerk of a boyfriend, and supposedly they were both lost at sea. Presumed dead. I couldn't accept my sister was gone. You see, I'm the oldest, she's the middle, and we have a younger sister named Charlotte. She's the free spirit."

Melinda sat quietly for a moment, sipping her wine, a look of intense concentration upon her lovely, unmarked face.

"When I heard what happened, I went to England. I looked all over the castle grounds and in the local village, but I couldn't find any trace of her. The authorities were useless. So I went back home to try to get on with my life. Only I couldn't."

"You are not French, and I'll wager you are not Scottish or Welsh. Where are you from?"

His gaze was drawn to her mouth when she bit her lip.

"My country hasn't been discovered yet. It won't be until 1492. It's called America. I come from the state of North Carolina. From a town called Holden Beach. It's hot in the summer and the sea air here reminds me of home. It smells similar here, except colder and older, if that makes any sense."

James knew exactly what she meant. For he loved living by the sea. The scent of the ocean eased his mind. A servant came in to build up the fire. When the child left, James propped his chin on his fists.

"Continue your tale."

"So you see, I tried to get on with my life, but then something happened that made me think she wasn't really dead."

He couldn't help it—he leaned forward in the chair, curious as to what she would say.

"I decided I was going to travel to England one last time.

Take a look around, and if I couldn't find any answers, I would finally accept Lucy's death and return home and get on with my life. But on the way to the airport—"

She paused as if considering what to tell him. He watched her closely, looking for any sign she was lying. Melinda nodded to herself.

"The airport is a place you go to book passage. Except it's not a horse or a carriage. It's like a large metal bird that flies in the sky. You climb inside, fly in the sky over the ocean, and in eight hours or so you arrive in England. I know that's fast, but I swear it seems to take forever."

He gaped at her. "Metal birds? Eight hours to cross an ocean?"

"That's the best way I can think of to describe a plane. Yes, people can fly through the air."

"Are you afraid you will fall from the sky?" Not that James believed her; he was merely curious to hear her tale.

"Well, I think when airplanes were first invented people were afraid they would fall out of the sky. But they've been around for such a long time people think of them like you think of horses. No big deal. Although seriously, horses scare me more than airplanes. I'm always afraid the horse is going to bite me or kick me."

James frowned severely. "You traveled in one of these flying birds to England." Witless girl. He would not hurt her tender feelings. 'Twas the reason he listened to her tale. Truly.

"Then what transpired?"

"Before I traveled in the plane, I was driving... A car is

like a horse made of metal, but it doesn't look like an actual horse. More like a box. You don't feed it—well, you put gas in it..." She waved a hand. "Never mind. You sit inside the horseless carriage and drive. The car can take you across long distances very quickly. Not as fast as an airplane, but fast."

"A metal carriage?"

She held up a hand. "I'll tell you all about various modes of transportation later. Let me get the story out before I lose my nerve."

He sat back and waited, curiosity spiraling through his body. He hadn't been as intrigued in... Well, he couldn't remember how long.

"So I was driving my car to the airport when out of nowhere another car crashed into my car. It was a terrible crash. I was hurt very badly. There was a man. He stood over me. He was English. The man told me he had been sent to kill me. Said once he killed me he would kill my other sister, Charlotte. And told me he was hired by a client to make sure Lucy was dead."

Anger coursed through James. He wanted to find this man and cleave his head from his shoulders. But he said not a word out loud. What would it be like to have a woman as fierce and passionate as Melinda to wife? He scowled. She was beautiful, and likely many chivalrous fools fought for her affection. She would not want a beast.

"I ended up in the hospital. The doctor said I was lucky to be alive. That was after I was in a coma...where you sleep and no one can wake you up. Five months passed. When I woke, I knew I had to go back. To search for answers."

She stared into the fire, and it seemed a spell encircled them. James needed to hear the rest of her story. The sound of her voice, her strange accent, made him feel comforted, enveloped in warmth.

"When I left the hospital and went home, I made arrangements to go back to England. I was on my way to the castle and somehow I turned left when I should have turned right and ended up here. At Falconburg. Only in my time, the castle is a ruin. It doesn't last."

She clapped her hand over her mouth. "I'm so sorry. I shouldn't have said that."

"My bones will have turned to dust in seven hundred years. I know I will never have children. I am the last of my line. When I die there will be nothing left. No one to carry on the Rivers name. Mayhap 'tis fitting Falconburg falls to ruin."

He thought for a moment. "Do other castles stand in your time?"

She nodded. "There are many castles still standing. Though it's become so expensive to own them. The National Trust manages them, or the family has to allow people to look at the castle. They pay money to walk around the castle."

James shuddered, imagining hordes of people gaping at the beast of Falconburg.

"I would not allow strangers in my home."

James watched the emotions cross her face. She looked as if she were deciding whether to tell him something.

"I was wandering around London and I went into a museum. There was a painting on the wall. One of many down a long hallway. The painting was from the fourteenth century."

She put her face in her hands, and he watched her shoulders shake, feeling helpless to aid her. There was a warrior within Melinda Merriweather. Did she know how strong she was to attempt such a journey alone? He admired her spirit.

"The painting was of a man, a woman, and five children. This is where things take a turn into strangeness. The woman in the painting—was my sister, Lucy."

She looked at him, anguish in her eyes, and in that moment James wanted to believe her. Found himself yearning to believe in her. To believe in anything.

"Mayhap the woman in the painting merely looked like your sister."

"Charlotte thought so. It's possible, but I believe it's her. At Blackford I found a letter. The sea air had turned most of it to dust, but I made out the word *safe*. It was Lucy's handwriting. As if she tried to leave me a message. I have to find Lucy. I don't know how or why, but I did travel through time. Now here I am in 1327. The problem is, I don't know *when* Lucy came back. I don't know what year. If it is her in the painting, then I know it was during this century, but nothing more. So I have no idea how to find her other than to go to Blackford Castle, where she was last seen."

Blackford Castle? The home of his enemy. James wanted to aid her, but taking her to Blackford was not possible.

Could he truly believe she was from the future? And not only her but also her sister? Or was it a ruse?

"If you truly are from the future, tell me of events to come."

She tilted her head. "Edward III is king, correct?"

He nodded.

"In ten years a famous war will start. It's called the Hundred Years War and is between England and France for control of the French throne."

James could no longer fight due to his injury. He sent men and gold in his stead. A war lasting a hundred years would bankrupt the nobles.

"And a terrible plague is coming. It's called the Black Plague. It hits London around 1348 and kills over twenty million people across Europe. It's spread by fleas and rats."

She shuddered, and a chill passed through the room.

"Then we shall keep cats at Falconburg." Dolt. He made a strangled sound.

"It's a terrible death." She looked grim.

"When I find Lucy, I'm going to smack her. Why didn't she try to preserve the letter in better condition?"

Melinda placed a hand on his arm. Heat from her touch traveled to his heart. She looked him in the eye when she spoke. Did not flinch from his visage.

"Do you know Lord Blackford? It's the last place Lucy visited. I need to see if anyone there knows her."

Melinda clenched her fists. "You have to understand. The scarf that man from the market was wearing, it's a pattern my sister came up with. I have to leave now. See what they know about Lucy. Will you help me?"

"I will not take you to such a wretched place. The Brandons are my mortal enemy. I would see William, now Lord Blackford, dead, along with his entire line."

Melinda took three steps back. He knew he was scaring her. He threw the goblet into the fire, snarling.

"You will obey my command and stay here. I will send a spy to inquire about your sister." James pinched the bridge of his nose and swore viciously. "Now leave me, woman."

Chapter Thirteen

James leaned back in the chair. William Brandon. He hated the man with a passion. 'Twas he who'd massacred James' entire family in a dispute over lands so many years ago. Because of him, James was the last of his name.

It must have been a score of years ago when William Brandon was awarded Blackford Castle on the coast of the North Sea. If he had the chance, James would kill Lord Blackford without a moment's hesitation.

He was but a babe when it happened. James was the youngest at two years old. Theirs was a loving family. He had two older sisters and three older brothers. His mother and father loved each other very much. While theirs was an arranged marriage, they'd fallen deeply in love. At least, that was what the servants told him.

A hazy memory of walking through blood filled his dreams. Another was the sound of laughter—he thought perhaps 'twas his parents' laughter. A distant cousin arrived at Falconburg. Took him home to raise James as a son. A powerful lord of few words. When he heard James crying himself to sleep, he used to say, "Crying doesn't help." He'd never had the guts to tell his cousin crying made him feel better. Instead he'd learned to suppress his emotions.

When William murdered his family, Falconburg and its inhabitants were engaged in a feud with the Brandons. His father's trusted advisor had told James that William killed his oldest brother during a battle, starting the feud. His other brother Henry swore it had been done in a cowardly fashion. He didn't know exactly what happened—only that William and his mercenaries had massacred James' entire family. The only reason he was spared was because a trusted servant hid him in a chest at the foot of her bed. In the aftermath, one of the servants found him trying to wake his father, covered in blood.

A few years later, William wed a strange wench. There was talk of the lady being a witch. No one knew where she'd come from. Who her people were.

And now Melinda Merriweather appeared on his lands. Coincidence? James didn't believe in coincidence. He could not deny the strange manner of speech and Melinda's odd ways.

The story she told him of traveling from the future—was it possible? Could she be from the future? And if so, did that mean her sister Lucy was also from the future?

From what James knew, Lady Blackford had married William a score of years ago. How could she be Melinda's sister? Melinda was very young.

The thought of burying his blades deep within William's heart pleased him. Then he scowled and stomped around the solar. If he went to Blackford, William would see his scarred face. Mark his injuries. James would appear weak.

"Well? When do we leave?"

"I told you to leave me be, woman."

He scowled at the woman in front of him.

"Oh, is that what you said? I thought you wanted me to fetch more wine." She held up a jug.

If he could heal, they could go in the spring. It would give him time to plan his revenge.

"The weather is too treacherous to make the journey. We will make the journey in the spring."

"Spring? The hell if I'm waiting till spring. I have to go now. Don't you understand? That woman could be my sister. You don't know what I've gone through."

"You will not argue with me, wench."

Her head came up to his chin. She stood so close to him that James could see flecks of gold in her green eyes. Right now they were narrowed at him. Her skin turned a fetching shade of strawberry. She looked beautiful. He wanted to take her in his arms.

James shook himself. If she was the sister of Lady Blackford, Melinda had been sent here to spy on him. He could not trust her.

"Wench? You are an arrogant, insufferable jerk. Who are you to tell me what to do? I'm going. I don't give a fig what you say."

James shut his mouth with a snap. Never in his life had a

woman argued with him. His word was law. Yet Melinda Merriweather stood up to him like the fiercest warrior and bellowed. He suppressed the beginnings of a smile. He liked her feisty nature. She wasn't afraid of him, even though he looked like a monster.

Melinda slammed the door behind her as she left. James stood staring into the fire, pondering what to do. He best have his men watch her. Given her temper, she would try to find a way to go on her own. It was what he would do.

He went to the door, yanked it open, and bellowed down the hallway, "Renly."

Renly skidded to a stop in front of him, out of breath from running.

"My lord?"

"Have two of the men watch over Mistress Merriweather. Make sure she doesn't try to filch a horse from the stables."

His captain arched a brow but refrained from speaking. Instead the man turned on his heel and left the room.

James might admire her spirit, but he would go no further with his feelings. He would not allow himself to care for the sister of a Brandon.

The nerve! Melinda stomped around the chamber. If that insufferable, arrogant ass thought he could tell her what to do, he was sadly mistaken.

Melinda wanted to throw something, but there were so few items in the room that she leaned into the covers and screamed.

She planned to go down and eat dinner. But when she walked into the great hall and saw James sitting at the table talking with his men, she was afraid she would scream at him if she stayed.

So the weather was bad—so what? She understood it wasn't like getting in a car and driving, worrying if the roads were clear. The few roads she'd seen were basically mud. But still. The thought of Lucy being on the other coast was enough to make her crazy. Melinda wasn't going to wait. She kept to the edge of the hall, making her way to the kitchens.

She said hello to the cook. "I'm rather tired. I think I'll take dinner in my room."

The cook nodded, and Melinda was left to fix a platter while servants scurried to and fro. She made sure to take extra for her road trip.

Back in the room, she ate dinner and planned. Anger didn't help. As much as she wanted to storm and stomp around the room, she had to focus.

There was no way she could leave at night. The gates would be closed, not to mention her horrible sense of direction. She'd get a good night's sleep and leave in the morning. With everyone coming and going, she could slip out unnoticed.

Chapter Fourteen

In the morning, Melinda woke with a headache. She'd spent a restless night dreaming of Lucy. In her dream she made it to Blackford Castle only to find the woman was not Lucy. In another dream, she made it to the castle to find she was too late and her sister died years ago. And in the third dream, she never made it to the castle, dying along the way. That one made her shudder.

She didn't have any kind of suitcase or bag. Hands on her hips, she turned, surveying the room. It would have to do. Melinda pulled the sheet off the bed. Within it she put her future clothes, as she'd come to call them, and the food she'd squirreled away. She tied up the bedsheet into a makeshift satchel, one she could loop over her shoulder.

One of the knights would notice it. Melinda hiked up her skirts and tied the satchel around her waist. With her cloak on, she didn't think anyone would notice. She put two carrots she'd swiped in the top of her boot. One of her hair ribbons kept them from falling down the boot. Satisfied, she made her way down the stairs, looking like she knew where she was going.

James and his men were fighting in the lists, hurling insults back and forth. She paused for a moment to watch. He was a sight. Fighting with two swords, the man was all grace and power. Even injured, he made swordplay look like anyone could do it. As she watched him, she realized all the movies she'd seen, all the books she'd read, didn't do the real thing justice. He was graceful, and yet she knew those swords could take your head off in one swipe.

He was going to be angry when he found out what she'd done. Maybe not that she'd left, but definitely angry she'd taken his horse. Melinda chuckled to herself. She was going to take the big black horse. She thought she'd heard it called a warhorse.

The beast was huge, but for some reason he liked her. So she made sure to visit whenever she went outside. And she knew the horse liked carrots. James might be unreasonable, but at least his horse was nice.

When she arrived at the stables, she walked in like she owned the place. A sigh of relief left her lips. Instead of the usual assortment of men and boys working, there were only two young boys on duty. She squared her shoulders and walked up to them.

"Lord Falconburg says I can take his horse for a ride." She took a carrot out of her pocket and made kissing noises at the big black animal. He pricked up his ears and came forward. He took the carrot from her, his velvety muzzle rubbing her hand.

One of the boys scratched his head. "Nay, mistress. My lord does not allow anyone to ride his horse." He eyed her nervously. "He's a foul-tempered beast."

"The horse or his master?"

Melinda had the satisfaction of seeing the boy's mouth drop open. She felt a little mean, but not enough to feel bad about it.

The boy started to argue but she cut him off. "Do you want to interrupt Lord Falconburg while he's in the lists, or will you get out of my way and let me take the horse for a ride?"

The other boy said, "Let her go."

The first boy looked at him dubiously but shrugged and helped her saddle the horse.

Melinda leaned close and stroked the horse on his neck. While the boys were getting things ready, she discreetly pulled the satchel from underneath her skirts and secured it to the saddle.

She whispered, "Don't throw me off and you can have another carrot. I packed more in my bag for later." The horse flicked his ear, and she took it as a sign he wouldn't bite or kick her.

Wow, talk about being up high. Melinda swallowed and looked down at the ground. It seemed like an awful long way to fall. The horse twitched, and she realized she shouldn't show fear. Didn't they say horses could sense fear? So she sat up straight and urged the horse forward. He was obviously well trained, because she didn't know what she was doing but the horse seemed to understand she wanted to go forward, and obliged.

She rode through the gates like she had every right. Melinda even managed a wave to the guardsmen leaning negligently over the gate. So far it was shaping up to be a good morning. She'd given the two men assigned to her the slip early this morning. One of them she didn't really give the slip; more like she locked him in the garderobe. But he was sort of a jerk and deserved it. The other man had a crush on one of the serving girls from the kitchen.

The girl liked him too. So Melinda had pulled the girl aside and said the man had been asking about her. The girl's eyes lit up, and the next thing she knew, Melinda spotted her with the man in an alcove, kissing. She had one moment wondering what it would be like to kiss James before shoving the thought away. She couldn't stay here. She had to get to Blackford and find out if Lucy was there.

Melinda swore she held her breath all the way through the gates until she was clear of the castle.

"Okay, we made it this far. Now which way?" The horse didn't answer. Melinda thought for a moment. When she was trying to get to Blackford before, she turned left when she should've turned right. So right it was. She tugged on the right rein and used her right knee, and easy-peasy, the horse went the way she wanted. Another good sign.

All she had to do was keep going in a straight line until she reached the coast. Castles were big. It shouldn't be hard to find. Even as a ruin, Blackford was pretty impressive. Melinda pictured what it must look like now, and thought she would definitely be able to see it from far away.

Chapter Fifteen

The horse ambled on through the morning. Melinda stopped twice to stretch and drink water from a stream. The third time she stopped to eat lunch. She gave the horse another carrot and a slightly wrinkled apple she'd found in the larder. There wasn't a tree or rock to tie the horse up.

"Don't go back home. Be a good horse and find some grass."

He seemed content, and she was happy to walk a bit and then sit without moving. As she was unused to riding a horse, her thighs ached and she felt like she was still moving whenever she dismounted. The muscles in her body weren't used to the movements required to mount, dismount, and ride. And to think she used to complain about sitting at a desk all day.

"Time to go, big boy." This time it only took three tries to get on the horse. Progress.

"Sorry about that, boy. Guess you can tell I'm not used to

riding. In my day the horses require a key and gas."

The horse flicked his ear. A horse of few words, just like his master. She didn't have a watch, but thought it was late afternoon. In the short time she'd been here, Melinda had noticed it would start growing dark before dinner. And by dinner it was definitely dark. If they stepped into a hole or got stuck in the mud, she'd be at the mercy of whoever happened along. No thank you. Melinda had had enough of being tied up and threatened.

The going hadn't been too bad. James was being unreasonable. She looked to the sky again.

"We'd better stop. I wouldn't want anything to happen to you."

Not only was the horse valuable, but she liked the big black beast. Suddenly it dawned on her. The sound she'd been hearing for a while was the ocean. Why on earth was she near the ocean? They should be going in the opposite direction. They rode on, and damned if Melinda didn't see water. She slid down from the saddle, stamping her foot.

"I swear I could get lost going home at night." She stroked the horse. "I know it isn't your fault. You were just going where I wanted to go. I wish you came with GPS." The horse snorted and shook his head.

It was too late to keep going. Oh well. She'd have to stop here. They'd basically gone in a giant circle.

She found shelter behind some rocks. Grass grew at the base. The horse quickly chowed down. Melinda had no idea how to start a fire. What she wouldn't give for matches or a lighter. Completely frustrated and shivering, she pulled the cloak tight around her, huddling against the rocks and the horse. He snuffled her hair and went back to eating.

"We have to ration the carrots until we come across a town or somewhere we can buy more. Bon appétit."

A sliver of guilt ran through Melinda as she patted the pouch at her waist. She'd swiped a few coins off the desk in James' room to add to what he'd given her on market day. It wasn't like there was a cash machine close by. In all fairness, she'd left her earrings in return. They were small diamonds encircled by emeralds and sapphires. And while not worth a great deal, they should cover what she took. At least, she hoped it was a fair trade. She had no idea of the currency of the time.

The dress was cumbersome for riding. It was the devil to take on and off by herself. She knew; she'd tried it one night. Looked like she'd be sleeping fully clothed, especially since she couldn't make a fire. She pulled her necklace out, holding the charms in her palm. The necklace had belonged to Aunt Pittypat. It was a heavy gold chain with four charms. There was an emerald, a diamond, a sapphire, and one gold charm in the shape of the unicorn.

Melinda tucked it back under her shirt for safekeeping. There was a stream nearby where she refilled the earthenware jug she was carrying. It seemed like they were always passing a small stream or other body of water. Kind of like a medieval water fountain. She'd washed under the fabric as best she could. The salted beef she'd eaten for dinner tasted sort of like beef jerky. It was filling but made her thirsty.

Resigned to being cold, she curled up in the cloak and sent up a prayer that horse wouldn't run off. She wrapped the reins around her legs, but had no doubt if the horse wanted to leave, he could.

"Leave me alone. I'm sleeping." Melinda woke slowly. She was having the most decadent dream. In it, she was in a huge white bed, surrounded by pillows and eating a bagel with cream cheese and lox. And drinking hot chocolate while the latest Daniel Craig movie played. In the dream, someone brought her a Bloody Mary. Before she could take a sip, the dream crumbled. She was cranky on the best mornings, but this took the cake. Melinda opened her eyes and glared. "What?"

Chapter Sixteen

Three men stood in front of Melinda. One of them held the horse's reins in his hands.

"You have got to be kidding me." She wanted to groan. Not again. "Drop the reins and leave now and I won't turn y'all into toads."

Two of the men crossed themselves, and she resisted the urge to laugh. She needed them to be afraid of her so they would go on their way. She didn't have time for this. Blackford Castle and Lucy were within her grasp.

Apparently the third man wasn't afraid of being turned into a frog. He barked orders to the other men. They grabbed hold of her as she struggled, screaming and kicking. Her foot made contact with one of the men's noses, and she was gratified to hear the crunching sound. A copper smell filled the air.

Good. She hoped she'd busted his nose. Satisfaction coursed through her. But it was short-lived. They threw her over the back of the horse, leading him down a path toward the rocky beach. The horse bared his teeth to bite. One of the men yanked hard on the reins and the animal settled down.

"The horse belongs to Lord Falconburg. You better leave him with me. If I don't return with him soon, he'll come looking."

Two of the men looked nervous until their leader shrugged. "Lord Falconburg will have to catch us first, lady."

She looked at each face, memorizing what they looked like and what they were wearing. If she survived and James didn't kill her for losing his best horse, she wanted to be able to tell him what the thieves looked like. Wanted to be there when he caught them. Was she becoming a barbarian? Melinda never considered herself prone to violence, but ever since she'd arrived in the fourteenth century, where she found herself thrust into one situation after another, she'd changed her mind. And right about now, as angry as she was, she'd cheer when James skewered them like big ole shish-kabobs.

They were all wet from the spray striking the rocks. At the base of the cliff where the water met the shore, they led her around a group of rocks and into what looked like a passageway or cave. You wouldn't know it was there unless you were right on top of it. The entrance was tucked into a corner of the rock. Were they smugglers?

Inside the dark cave, one man lit a torch. For a moment she envied him and opened her mouth to ask how before she remembered she was not a guest but a prisoner. The dim light cast shadows on the stone walls. On the back wall she saw iron rings. Maybe they were used to pull the boats in?

Panic rose within her as the men pulled her arms above her head.

"Let me go and I won't tell Lord Falconburg there are smugglers using his beaches."

The men laughed. They tied her tightly to the rings. They were as thick as her wrist and there was no slack in the rope. The leader leaned close to her. The smell of alcohol was so strong Melinda wondered if you could get a contact buzz.

"The horse is mine. He'll bring a fine price. 'Tis low tide now. When the water rises, you'll drown. If you don't die of cold first."

The leader gestured to the other man. They were leaving her here alone. Melinda screamed for all she was worth.

One of the men turned around. "Witches can't abide salt water."

"I'm no witch, idiot. Let me go and I'll ask Lord Falconburg not to kill you."

"The Red Knight has changed. He is a deformed beast who eats women and children. He will not save you."

The leader grabbed her around the waist, pulling her close. The ropes cut into her wrists, the boots protecting her ankles from the rough rope.

"Shall we get to know the lady better?"

There was no effing way. "Lay one finger on me and I will make your man parts shrivel and fall off."

The man backed away from her, a look of horror on his

face. She bit her lip to keep from laughing.

"I won't curse you if you free me now."

The man seemed to be deciding, but shook his head. "You are a witch. Cast a spell and free yourself."

He stood with his arms crossed over his chest. The other two looked fearful. One seemed to be muttering prayers.

When nothing happened, he grinned. "Let the water take ye, witch." One of the men crossed himself. "Scream as loud as you like. No one will hear you."

As they left, Melinda watched her meager belongings leave on the back of the horse. Someone had to come by. The rings looked well used. Melinda screamed until she was hoarse. There was no way anyone would hear her over the waves crashing against the rocks.

Water trickled into the cave. Tiny streams formed, then a puddle, and now it was over her ankles. Melinda pulled against the rope as hard as she could, but it was no use. The rings wouldn't budge. How many people died this way?

In looking at the water stains on the wall inside the cave, a sense of impending doom rose within her. The cave would be completely submerged at high tide.

Why had she traveled over seven hundred years only to drown in a cave? As the water rose, Melinda's teeth quit chattering. How long until she died of hypothermia? Time seemed to be speeding up. With each wave, the water rose. Higher and higher. She must've passed out from the cold. A wave hit her in the face, waking her. The water was to her waist.

Had she come all this way only to die in medieval

England without finding Lucy? Melinda spent a lot of time thinking about what would happen when she made it back to the future. While she hadn't found it yet, she was sure love was waiting around a corner. The kind of epic love she'd read about in books. So powerful she'd thought about the characters for days or weeks after she'd finished the story. That was what she wanted in life. She didn't care what anyone said, Melinda believed in true love with all her heart.

She closed her eyes. "I wish to get out of here and find my own happily ever after."

Chapter Seventeen

James would not tolerate a shrewish tongue or disordered curls. And especially not eyes the color of emeralds. His gaze fell upon the ring lying on top of the desk. 'Twas a family ring. The large sapphire reminded him of her. Mysterious and full of hidden depth.

Flowers and vines carved into the band reminded him of her wanton curls. His finger had healed crookedly and the ring would no longer slide all the way down. He hoped in time it would fit again. James tried it on his right hand. It slipped over the knuckle, fitting perfectly. He laid it back on the desk with a thud. No—he would not wear it again until he was whole. His boot hit the wall, and James cursed. Mayhap he would never wear the ring again. Her face would likely haunt him for a very long time indeed.

The cheek of the lass. Melinda Merriweather had run off and gravely insulted him by stealing his favorite warhorse. She'd spent the previous night in her chamber. James had left her alone to her womanly thoughts but when he didn't see her the next day, he inquired of the servants. No one had seen her. A small boy from the stables came forward.

"I'm awfully sorry, my lord." The boy looked at the ground, kicking at the dirt. "Mistress Merriweather said you wanted her to take your horse for a ride. I knew you didn't let anyone ride him, but she can be very fearsome."

James rolled his eyes. He could imagine her standing there, hands on her hips, intimidating the boy into giving her what she wanted.

"The horse went willingly? He did not bite her?"

The boy nodded vigorously. "She gave him carrots. He liked them very much."

James should have known she'd find a way to leave. He snorted. The bloody horse could be bought with a simple carrot. Melinda was a full day ahead of him. Several of the men rode with him as he set off on his second-best horse to find her. She was no doubt headed for Blackford. James would have to show his deformed face. Listen to William's taunts. He scowled. Let him yap like a dog. James would take his head.

One of the men rode back to James. "My lord, 'tis passing strange—the tracks lead in the wrong direction."

He could not keep the smile from his face. She was traveling north, not east. If Melinda continued, she would eventually arrive in Scotland. He could not imagine she meant to travel to the land of barbarians. The smile turned to a frown. Unless she were a spy and plotted to meet her master.

"We follow." Was it too much to ask for a meek and quiet girl? One he could get with an heir and a spare, then leave her behind tending his home whilst he went back where he belonged, to battle.

What else was there? He craved the thrill of battle. The clanging of swords. If James was no longer a warrior, he was nothing. The wounds on his body healed slowly, paining him greatly. He shifted in the saddle to ease the ache, grateful when they stopped to eat midday.

James eased himself off the horse, his left leg giving way. He managed to catch himself and leaned against the horse until his leg would hold his weight. He would not fall in front of the men. They knew what had happened to him. Had seen the terrible injuries. Renly and three others had carried him from the battlefield.

'Twas the most grievous insult to be told by the healer and his sovereign he could no longer fight. To know he was less. Would never be whole. All that was required of him now was to provide men and gold as his sovereign required.

They traveled the rest of the day, following the tracks.

Renly chuckled. "Seems the lady is going in a circle."

The tracks ended at the cliffs. For a moment James could not breathe, imagining her broken on the rocks. He dismounted and walked to the edge. Relief swept through him. There was no sign of her or his horse. No sign they had fallen over the edge in the dim light. No fallen stones or debris. The tide was rising, and it would be dark soon.

His best tracker stood before him, discomfited. "The lady traveled in a circle. Wandering, as if she had no idea where to go."

So she wasn't riding for Scotland. It seemed she didn't know where she was going. Blackford was the opposite direction. Couldn't they find their way in the future? James shook his head, unwilling to believe her fantastical tale of time travel.

One of his knights approached. "There are trees near. We can make camp."

There were other tracks nearby. James peered down at a set of tracks. Renly knelt down.

"'Tis the big black. See the mark here? He got it...in the last battle, my lord."

It went without saying he meant the battle where James and his horse were injured. So his horse was nearby and traveling with others. Had Melinda met her master? James would discover the enemies plotting against him. What coward sent a woman to do their work?

"We follow. Find the lady."

The men mounted up, keeping silent, following the tracks. They came to a small clearing. James signaled the men to keep quiet. They dismounted and tied the horses to the trees, making their way on foot. James sent up a prayer his leg would hold. For he intended to destroy his enemy. And Melinda? James didn't hold with killing women. He wasn't sure what to do with her. A small part of his mind told him to make her his own, the spoils of the fight. But he could never trust her. And he needed a woman unafraid of him; one he could trust.

There were five men. One with a broken nose, another

with a black eye. Melinda's handiwork, no doubt. Pride swelled in his breast. The lady had a temper to match her hair. But where was she? He saw no sign. His horse stood with the others, ear twitching. The animal raised his head and let out a low nicker. James shook his head and the horse went back to eating.

His men approached stealthily so they surrounded the men. James stepped into the firelight. The man with the black eye leapt up, drawing a sword.

"You dare to steal from the Red Knight." James pointed to the horse. "Where is the rider?"

The rest of his men stepped into the firelight, hands on the hilts of their swords.

The man with the broken nose spat. "The wench is dead."

Red rage washed over James. Instinct made him draw his blades. With one fluid motion, the man no longer had a head. He flipped the blades up, resting them on his shoulders.

"What happened to her?"

One of the other men reached for a bow and soon found himself with a blade to the chest courtesy of one of James' knights.

Three ruffians remained. One tried to run and was cut down. James was in no mood to take prisoners. For killing Melinda, they would all die this night. He was within his right to kill them for stealing his horse. He wanted to make them suffer for taking the one woman left in the realm who could look him in the eye without flinching. The man with the black eye dropped his sword.

"The witch wasn't worth the trouble. We took her horse and left her to die as an evil one should. Cleansed by salt water."

Ice formed across James body. They'd drowned her?

He pointed a blade at the man's neck, noting the red drops welling under the tip of the blade. James brought the sword up, forcing the man to look him in the eye.

"Tell me now and I'll grant you a quick death."

The man gulped. "She's in the cave. We tied her to the wall. By now the tide is high. She is drowned. The witch tried to put a curse on us."

James ended the man with one thrust of the blade. As he sheathed his swords, he looked around. The five men lay dead around the fire.

"Take the horses."

There was a fallen tree nearby. James stepped on it to mount the horse.

"To me." He urged the horse to a gallop, his men following. Was he too late? Had he failed her? James wouldn't think on it. He urged the horse forward, faster.

The wind shifted and he thought he heard her cry out. He and Renly scrambled down the side of the rocks. The rest of the man stayed with the horses in case any other danger was close by.

He heard his captain suck in a breath. "James, 'tis too late. Look to the entrance."

James eyed the opening of the cave, the water close to the top. He turned to Renly. "If I do not make it out, take care of the men."

James removed his cloak, leaving one of his swords and knives behind. He took the other sword and knife and dove deep into the water. He couldn't see very well; the salt water turned everything a murky green. The water chilled him through as he swam through the opening. He came up with his head a few feet from the roof.

"Melinda!"

He heard coughing.

"Over here." Her voice was weak.

She struggled to keep her head above water. James went under, could feel both her hands and legs fastened to iron rings set in the wall. With the knife, he cut the ropes binding her legs and came up for air.

"Please don't let me drown."

"Take a deep breath." James watched the next wave wash over her face and knew he was out of time. He dove again, cutting through the ropes binding her hands.

She was sinking. James grabbed her around the waist and swam, using all his strength. Strength he didn't know he had left within his body. He pulled Melinda through the opening. Renly and the men waited to help. One of the men threw a rope down. James tied it around Melinda's waist and they pulled her up. James climbed up the rocks, ignoring the pain burning through his body. As he neared the top, two of the men reached down and pulled him over the edge. He lay there gasping.

Melinda was as pale as the moon. She wasn't moving. James rolled onto his knees and crawled over to her.

"Don't go, love. You must wake."

He turned her on the side, pounding on her back, as he'd seen done to men who almost drowned in the past. Living by the sea, one learned to swim as a child. Everyone knew someone the sea swept away to a watery grave.

She started to cough and retched up seawater. James continued to pat her on the back until she expelled all the water.

He tried to lift her up, but his leg gave way. "Bloody hell."

"Let me take her," his captain said.

Another man helped James up on the horse. 'Twas all he could do to stay upright in the saddle. Renly lifted Melinda, helping her onto the horse and James pulled her close.

"Don't ever do that again. Methinks you almost killed me, lady."

She tilted her face up to him.

"Don't worry. I have no intention of ever drowning."

He stroked her hair.

"Did the men. Did they—defile you?"

She rolled her eyes at him, teeth chattering.

"I'm fine... Well, other than almost drowning. I told them I'd put a hex on them and make their man parts fall off if they touched me."

His men crossed themselves. James threw back his head and laughed. A rusty, grating sound, but a laugh nonetheless. Seemed only Melinda Merriweather could make him smile.

Chapter Eighteen

The sound emanating from James' mouth startled Melinda. Was he choking? No. It was a laugh. It was the first time she'd heard him laugh, and it sounded like a cross between a rusty door squeaking and a hippo with a cold. The goofy sound coming out of such a serious man's mouth made her laugh as well. She sneezed three times and wished for a never-ending box of tissues.

"You are traveling north, lady, not east—unless you planned to travel to Scotland?"

Melinda twisted in the saddle to look at him. Once she knew he was watching her, she stuck her tongue out at him.

"I'm the absolute worst with directions. It's something of a Merriweather curse. All of my sisters have a terrible sense of direction. One time, Charlotte, she's my youngest sister, was on her way home and there was an accident. In taking a detour, she got lost and ended up two towns away."

She pulled the cloak more tightly around her and

sneezed again. Her head ached and she couldn't feel her toes. Part of her was detached, taking in the scenery, and the other part wanted a hot bath and to sleep for a week. In her mind there was nothing worse than having a cold. She'd rather be sick for a few days than deal with a cold that could last for a week, easy. Melinda knew she was the most awful patient. All she needed was a good meal, a cup of spiced wine, and a hot bath. She'd sell her soul for a pitcher of fresh-squeezed orange juice. A good night's sleep and she would be fine. There was no time to get sick; she had things to do and places to go.

When she told him how awful she was with directions, James actually smiled, a full-on smile with teeth showing. It transformed his face. And he had straight white teeth. Melinda ran her tongue over her own teeth, thinking of all the yellowed smiles with rotted or missing teeth she'd seen since arriving. She'd heard the whispers around the castle. Seen the small girls running from him. Didn't they realize how their behavior must hurt his feelings? Just because he was a warrior didn't mean the man didn't have feelings. Melinda would break down and cry, likely never leave her house again, if people ran screaming from her. But James seemed to take it in stride, at least on the outside.

She leaned against his chest, the vibration of his heartbeat calming her.

"Why do you hate William? Is he really so terrible? Though after what happened with the last guy Lucy fell for, I better reserve judgment until I hear the story. It was all because of him she ended up in the past."

A fit of coughing racked her body before she could ask another question. James helpfully pounded her on the back. Hard enough to send her sliding off the horse. He caught her before she went over.

"Apologies."

She shook her head. "It's all right. Will you tell me about him?"

Sitting in front of James on the saddle, Melinda felt him flinch. Yes, she was curious about his past, and the longer he took to answer the more her imagination filled in the blanks. What if Lucy was with another man like Simon? Or held here against her will?

James spoke in a low tone, his breath warm against her ear.

"I was but a babe when it happened. William killed one of my brothers during a battle. My other brother said 'twas done on purpose. William stabbed my brother in the back. What happened on the battlefield that day unleashed a feud between our families. It ended when William and his men killed my parents, my brothers, and sisters. A servant hid me in the chest in the bedchamber. 'Tis the only reason I was spared."

She put a hand on his thigh. "I'm so sorry. To grow up without family is a terrible thing. And to know the man responsible is free. I would want him to pay for what he did."

"William Brandon *will* pay."

"My sister is with some old man? We have to save her from him. She wouldn't be with a horrible man unless he's holding her against her will. Do you think he forced her to marry him?"

The story James told her ratcheted up her worry. She needed to leave in the morning for Blackford Castle.

"How long ago did you lose your family?"

"A score of years."

"Is that ten?"

She could feel the vibrations through James' chest as he spoke. She liked listening to his voice. The accent was yummy, but it was the depth of his voice that made her feel safe.

"A score of years is twenty, lady."

"I was right, then—William Brandon is a dirty old man."

James actually chuckled. "He is forty...mayhap forty-five years old, though I'm told he's in remarkable health for a man his age. Still fights for the king in battle."

Melinda couldn't imagine being with a man twenty years older than she. And there was no way Lucy would. She didn't like older men. Always dated men her own age or very close. Something didn't add up.

"What would you do, lady? Would you slay an entire family?"

For a moment she didn't answer. Her ex-boyfriend Carl used to say he loved her looks, so she didn't need to speak. He thought she was dumb, never asked her opinion. James asked her what she thought. Seemed interested in the answer.

"I think you can only guess what you would do. Unless you're actually in the situation. I would like to think I'd be rational enough to talk through what happened. But I'm not sure. I have a bit of a temper."

James laughed again, his odd-sounding laugh. "Aye, lady. You have a fearsome temper."

She elbowed him in the stomach and smirked when he let out a grunt. Another fit of coughing racked her body.

"The thing is, we don't know why William killed your brother. Maybe William is a jerk and relishes killing people. Then again, could there have been something else going on? We weren't there, so we don't know the truth. I swear, I will take your sword and kill him myself if he's harmed my sister."

Back at the castle, James tended to the horses while Melinda sipped a cup of spiced wine and nibbled on a bit of bread. The fires burning in the kitchen made it toasty, but she couldn't get warm. Mrs. Black told her to stay put while the servants heated water for the bath. Her head hurt, she had the sniffles, and she kept coughing and sneezing.

Given how many times she'd ended up soaking wet outside in the cold, Melinda shouldn't be surprised she'd caught a cold or maybe the flu. She'd hoped the cold virus was different in the past and she'd be immune. Wishful thinking. If only she had Aunt Pittypat's tried-and-true, never-fail hot toddy recipe. A cup of hot tea with a splash of whiskey, a spoonful of honey, and squeeze of lemon always worked wonders. Drink the concoction several times a day for a couple days and she'd be back on her feet feeling healthy again.

Her aunt would've loved traveling back in time. She was always up for new adventures. Melinda could picture her on the battlements under a full moon, dancing naked. Wherever her aunt was in her journey of the afterlife, Melinda knew she was having the time of her life. She reached to her neck, touching the necklace. Her aunt had never been one for material possessions. The necklace was all she had left. It was very precious to her.

Melinda soaked in the tub until her skin looked like a raisin. Mrs. Black brought her another dress. The gray one was ruined after ripping on the rocks and being in the salt water.

The dress was made of dark blue wool with embroidery around the hem and neckline. The chemise felt like linen. There was a matching blue ribbon to tie back her hair, and pretty stockings. She would wear her own boots. She felt very proper and presentable. Almost like she belonged. Imagine someone whose only job was to help you dress every day. Melinda couldn't fathom it.

Wrapped in a blanket, sipping another cup of wine, Melinda stared into the fire. Things were starting to look fuzzy. She wasn't a big drinker, so perhaps she was intoxicated. Though when she touched a hand to her forehead, the skin felt hot to the touch. Maybe it wasn't such a good idea to insist she was fine and wanted to dress. She better go to bed early.

"Mistress? Mrs. Black says you're wantin' to go to bed. Shall I help ye undress?"

Melinda must have dozed off. She wobbled a bit when she stood. "Thank you. I could never undo all these ties by myself."

The girl helped her out of her dress, leaving Melinda in her chemise. She was starting to like not worrying about undies and bras. The girl laid the ribbon on the table and brush out her hair.

"I'll fetch Mrs. Black. You're burning with fever, my lady."

The girl scurried out of the room. Too tired to care, Melinda crawled into bed and fell into a sleep fractured by nightmares.

Chapter Nineteen

Melinda woke feeling like she'd been run over by a truck. It was an effort to sit up in bed. Legs stretched out in front of him, James slept in the chair, chin resting on his chest. Trying to be quiet, she scooted back against the headboard to get a better look at him. He went out of his way to keep his face hidden. Asleep, she could look her fill.

He didn't believe her about being from the future. She couldn't really blame him. If a man showed up at Holden Beach dressed in tights and a long shirt and brandishing a sword, she would've called the closest hospital to come take him away. No way she'd talk to the crazy-pants guy. She would have gotten away from him as quickly as possible.

"Thank you for not throwing me in your dungeon," she whispered, not sure Falconburg had a dungeon but certainly hoping she'd never find out.

He had faint lines around the corners of his eyes. Probably from squinting against the sun. Though she liked to think they were laugh lines. And imagined him laughing and flirting. A hot slice of jealousy burned through her from thinking of him kissing all the pretty women. Bet they threw themselves at him by the dozens.

His face was dark with stubble, and her rescuer looked exhausted, with purplish circles under his eyes. He looked far older than twenty-two.

How many times had that crooked nose been broken? But it was the scar that ran through his eyebrow and eye, stopping beyond his cheekbone, that made her heart ache. He'd been incredibly lucky not to lose sight in the eye. Without thinking, Melinda reached out a finger to trace the scar. He shifted in the chair and she snatched her hand back under the covers.

The door to the chamber opened. Two servants bearing trays bustled in. The sound woke James instantly. His hand went to the sword at his hip. He was out of the chair, sword in one hand, knife in the other, before she blinked. When he saw who it was, he sat back in the chair with a wince.

The smell of freshly baked bread and—was that chicken potpie? It certainly smelled like it. Melinda's stomach growled. The corner of James' mouth twitched.

"How do you fare, Melinda?"

He'd called her by her first name. How could something so simple make her so happy? She'd told him he could do so when they'd met, but he'd insisted on calling her "mistress" or "lady" or "my lady." Or "wench" when he was displeased. What had changed?

"How long have I been sick? I must have had the flu."

He looked perplexed. Right, the word for flu must not exist yet. But he got her meaning, because he said, "You've been abed with a fever for a se'nnight."

"A week? Seriously? No wonder I'm so hungry." She threw back the covers. He put a hand on her shoulder.

"You are weak. Stay abed. I will serve you."

He smelled amazing. Like gingerbread and the ocean. Nope. They certainly didn't make guys like this in her time. At least none she'd encountered. Melinda leaned back against the pillows and waited. The straw mattress under the featherbed crackled when she moved. He brought her a cup of mead along with the food. She waited until he sat back down before she ate.

"This is so good." It was some kind of variation of chicken potpie. "Have you been here with me the entire time?"

He kept his eyes on his plate when he answered. "Aye. You gave the servants a fright." He smiled. She treasured each one, they were so rare.

"What happened? Did I do something embarrassing?"

"You were out of bed trying to climb out the window. Two of the men put you back in bed." He cocked his head. "They said they'd never heard such words from the mouth of a lady."

He was trying hard not to laugh. Melinda was mortified to think of the awful swearwords she knew thanks to Aunt Pittypat's eclectic group of friends.

James chuckled. "The men have taking a liking to your more inventive curses. I daresay there were many they'd never heard before."

She put her hands over her face, her cheeks hot. "I'm so sorry I caused any trouble. I don't remember any of it. All I remember were terrible dreams."

He looked grave. "After...my injuries, I too dreamt of terrible things while the fever held me close. Do not fret. I sent the men away and stayed with you."

James took her hand in his. She went still, feeling the rasp of the calluses on his palm as he stroked her hand. The muscles in his arm flexed beneath his tunic. The man was about six foot three, and every inch muscled. After seeing him in the lists and fighting to rescue her, she knew where the muscles came from.

James caught her staring at his scarred hand and snatched it away. She opened her mouth to protest then shut it. Calling attention to it would make him feel even more embarrassed. He'd obviously been a man used to showing affection. It was sad to think his injuries changed him so much. She would've liked seeing him before.

Strike that thought, said the green-eyed monster inside her. Melinda had the feeling before his injuries he wouldn't have given her the time of day. Well, he might have flirted with her like every other pretty woman he encountered. He probably fended off women lined up ten deep. Had his injuries softened him? She knew it was idle speculation. Usually she was a pretty good judge of character. Not counting a couple of ex-boyfriends. It seemed poor taste in men was another Merriweather curse. Aunt Pittypat married eight times before she passed.

"Will you tell me how you were injured?"

He leaned back in the chair. "'Twas during a battle. My injuries were so grave the healer said I would surely die." He crossed his booted feet at the ankles. "I was too stubborn to die."

James stopped speaking as a servant came in to clear the dishes.

"Do you require anything else, my lord?"

"That will be all."

When the man left, shutting the door behind him, James finished his wine. He stared into the fire for so long she wondered if he'd forgotten.

"After I healed enough to ride, I rode to claim my betrothed. She ran screaming from her father's hall. Before...there were many women who wished to wed me. I traveled to meet each eligible maiden. They were terrified by my face. Even here at Falconburg there are those who fear me."

Melinda's heart broke in two. She heard the pain in his voice, wanted nothing more than to make it go away. It wasn't pity; she was angry at those who'd destroyed his face. The violence made her think the wounds were inflicted on purpose.

"No woman in all the realm will wed the beast of Falconburg." The look of surprise must have shown on her face, for he said, "'Tis what they call me."

"They're hateful, silly women. Your looks are merely an outer shell. Looks fade as we age. They are ours to keep for only a short time. It's what is inside that counts."

Melinda could've said more, but she had a feeling she should give him small doses. If she told him she found him attractive, he wouldn't believe her. Lucy was her priority. Part of her yearned to see what would happen with James. A relationship? Something more? They'd only been together a short time, yet she knew more about him than anyone she'd ever dated. They spent all day together.

Melinda felt she'd known him forever. He was solid and steady. Not a man who would go chasing after another woman. A huge point in his favor: he listened to her, asked what she thought. And he didn't tell her a hundred times a day how beautiful she was. For that alone, Melinda would be forever grateful. Carl used to tell her she was like a painting, something pretty to look at, but of no substance.

Chapter Twenty

Three long, frustrating days passed before the healer pronounced Melinda healthy enough to travel. James stayed by her side night and day. She learned about his childhood, fostering with another family. While he told her it was normal for children to foster, she thought it sounded a bit sad and lonely. Melinda couldn't imagine being separated from her sisters at such a young age. Of course, he hadn't had a choice. To have your entire family taken from you at age two. The difficulty in remembering their faces and voices. Melinda was so thankful for the time she'd had with her family. She only hoped in finding Lucy they could go back. Not leave Charlotte alone in the world.

Yesterday James had walked with her through the gardens. New life appearing in the first flowers and plants. Tomorrow was April Fools' day. She'd been here almost a month. As she sat bundled up in blankets watching James and his men train in the lists, she had to admire the ferocity and grace with which they fought. Kind of like ballet with swords.

Back home... It was odd to keep thinking of it as the future. For it seemed now her future was here in the past. People always complained how busy they were. How stressed out. And the difficulties they faced. She shook her head. They had an easy life compared to these times. It wasn't like you could run to the grocery store and pick up a few things if you ran out. Here if you ran out during winter, you were out until spring.

James had told her of the years of bad harvests and how he tried to keep his people fed. She couldn't imagine going hungry. Sure, she'd gone on a few crazy fad diets, been so hungry she'd looked longingly at cardboard, but it was different. Hunger by choice wasn't the same when you could simply get in the car and drive to the store. Melinda knew there were children at home who went to school hungry. Relying on backpack programs and the local food pantry to ensure they had something to eat on the weekends. But here. She could see firsthand what it was like not to have enough.

It was harder living in the past. At the same time, there was a sense of purpose and peacefulness. The days had a rhythm. And while she'd always been a proponent of technology, Melinda found the lack of it strangely exhilarating. It was nice not to constantly check in and see what everyone else was doing on social media. Here no one called on the phone, wanting something. If you needed to talk to someone, you went to see them or you wrote a letter.

And letters could take ages before they were delivered, depending on the various hands they traveled through to reach their destination.

When she'd asked James if he'd heard back from the spy he sent to Blackford, he sat her down and explained how long it could take. She hadn't realized how long it took to do the simplest things. With a car, one could drive coast to coast in less than a day. The thought of traveling by horse to Blackford had her rubbing her backside.

"Mistress? My lord is ready."

She touched her necklace for good luck and followed the boy out of the solar, into the cold.

Melinda patted the big black horse. "I brought you a carrot. Now don't be jealous, I brought a carrot for my horse. I have to treat him nice too." The horse flicked his ear and nosed her hair. She kissed the side of the horse's face and whispered, "But you'll always be my favorite."

She eyed the dark brown horse. He wasn't as big as the black. James said the animal was even-tempered and wouldn't throw her. Comforting thought. She leaned close to the horse, whispering in his ear, "I hope bribes work with you too. How about a nice, tasty carrot?"

The horse happily munched his treat. A good sign. One of the boys helped her up on the horse, and she looked around the courtyard of the place she called home. Excitement filled her.

Finally. She would find out if Lucy was at Blackford. And if she wasn't, where was she? She knew deep in her gut that Lucy made the scarf. What were the chances people were crocheting here in England before it had been invented? Not likely.

If she found Lucy and they couldn't get back? Somehow they would leave clues for Charlotte and hope she would find them and also have the ability to travel through time. Melinda still didn't know how she'd done it. She'd ask Lucy what she thought. Between the two of them, they ought to be able to come up with a theory for Charlotte.

It was a punishing day riding through the rain. James watched Melinda for any sign she was unwell. She never complained. Not even as they rode through a stream and several muddy roads. He admired her spirit. The time he'd spent with her while she was unwell with fever, James would never tell anyone how he worried he was she would die. Melinda Merriweather was the only woman in the realm who looked upon him without making him feel she pitied him. She never flinched from his face.

Might she consider the beast of Falconburg for a husband? Hope had left him long ago, until she came into his life.

The ground was muddy and slow going for the horses. It would likely take them a fortnight to travel to Blackford. Plenty of time to think on his meeting with William Brandon.

James would not take Lord Blackford's head until Melinda found out if her sister were there. If she was Lady Blackford, she'd been so for a score of years. He'd seen many unhappy marriages. He stole a glance at Melinda. If her sister were anything like Melinda, James thought she would not accept remaining with a man who wasn't kind to her.

"Halt. We make camp here." It was early afternoon. James would've pushed on for several more miles, but Melinda looked tired. He still didn't believe her tale of traveling through time from the future, but he did know she was unused to riding. Children sat a horse better, yet she laughed and talked with his men, getting to know each one. The Red Knight and his fearsome warriors reduced to babes around the enchanting Melinda Merriweather.

"Thank the stars. I think my butt is numb."

His knights chuckled as Melinda stretched to ease her sore body.

James' leg did not pain him as much. He could now mount and dismount his horse without assistance. If only the scars on his face would disappear. William would take pleasure out of seeing the damage done to him.

When James had finished telling Melinda the story of his family, he wondered why Lord Blackford didn't seek him out and kill him. He knew James lived, was the Lord of Falconburg. Blood feuds lasted hundreds of years. It made no sense why his enemy would leave him alive these many years. Was it possible there was more to the story than his father's trusted advisor and servants had told him?

"I made sandwiches."

He looked at what Melinda held in her hands. It appeared to be two pieces of bread stuffed with cheese and fresh meat from the boar they'd killed and roasted before leaving Falconburg. James took a bite, chewed thoughtfully, and nodded.

"'Tis good. An easy way to eat while traveling. I never thought to put meat and cheese between bread."

One of the knights called out, "The mustard is what makes the food taste so good."

"No, 'tis the honey," another of the men said, chewing his sandwich.

Renly held up a hand. "Spicy and sweet together is the secret."

"You get the extra sandwich." Melinda handed James' captain the remaining morsel. James was jealous of food. What a dolt.

"The men do not believe she is a spy." Renly spoke in a low voice so she would not hear.

"Aye. Their stomach wants to believe." James watched her as she moved easily among the men.

"Then how did she come to be on my lands, alone? You see how she cannot find her way."

"Mayhap her story is true. I have oft wondered if there were truth to the stories of faeries and spirits."

James snorted. "You believe her tale?"

Renly looked at Melinda. She was singing a song to the men. It was unlike anything James ever heard, something about letting things go. The tune made him want to tap his feet.

"Aye. What she thinks shows on her face. If she were lying, we would know. Think you her sister is Lord Blackford's wife?"

"The Lady Blackford is old enough to be her mother. Melinda said her sister vanished at midsummer in the year 2015. And 'twas February 2016 when Melinda traveled through time. Her sister was twenty-four. But Lord Blackford's wife must be forty or forty-five, and 'tis said she was a beauty in her day with flowing brown hair. Look at Melinda's red hair. No, the Lady Blackford is not her sister."

"Mayhap they traveled to the past and ended up in different years?"

James thought about it. Who knew what powers were at work to bring a person through time? The explanation made sense. If it were true, Melinda would likely faint from fright when she saw her sister aged.

"Make sure the men are ready to kill Lord Blackford's guard when I give the word. I am undecided whether to talk to the man first or run him through and then talk."

Renly rested a hand on the hilt of his sword. "Kill them, not kill them. Makes no difference to me."

James pulled Melinda close as they bedded down for the night.

"You will catch an ague."

She yawned. "It's nice to sleep next to you, like having my own electric blanket." A soft sigh escaped her lips as she fell asleep.

What was "electric"? He noticed when she was tired or excited she spoke words he'd never heard before. For Melinda's sake, James would talk to William and then take the man's head. He was a man of reason. He would hear the tale from the lips of the man who had massacred his family. Then James would end William where he stood. And if it wasn't true? He didn't want to think upon all the years he'd wasted hating a man who perchance didn't deserve his hatred.

James rolled over and fell into an uneasy sleep, his dreams full of dark and evil things.

Chapter Twenty-One

After an entire week on the road, Melinda couldn't wait until tonight. James promised they would stay at an inn. Whenever she felt like complaining, she instead pictured rush-hour traffic. It worked every time. All the riding had either made her backside numb or she was finally getting used to so many hours a day on the back of a horse.

The snow slowed their progress. How quickly the things you fantasized about changed. Melinda used to fantasize about soaking in the tub, spending an entire day engrossed in a book, playing hooky and going to a movie during a rainy day, lazing on the beach all weekend during the summertime. Now...her greatest fantasy was a roof over her head, a dry place to sleep, and a warm and filling dinner. They'd been eating the wild boar the men had killed for days, and she was looking forward to a change.

The road trip allowed she and James to continue getting to know each other better. He didn't say much, a man of few words. And thought before he spoke. Melinda found him a refreshing change. The man was insightful and interesting. Best of all, he really listened to her. It was a new experience. One she could easily get used to.

As they rode into the courtyard of the inn, Melinda's knees buckled as she dismounted from the horse. James was there to catch her.

"Steady, Melinda."

Over the past week he'd called her by her first name. She felt like they'd crossed some sort of line, getting closer to each other ever since he had saved her from drowning and tended her while she was so sick. *You know you like him. Admit it.* Melinda pushed the feelings away.

She had to focus on finding Lucy before she could even think about a relationship, especially with someone more than seven hundred years older than she in medieval England. *Methinks the lady doth protest too much. In case you haven't noticed, you're already in a relationship.*

Shut up, voice.

Okay, technically she was older than him at twenty-six. He was only twenty-two. She was never one for dating younger men. It was fun to tease James, tell him he was 704 years older than her. Anyway, she wasn't staying in the past. Nope, she'd find Lucy and they would go back to Holden Beach and Charlotte. Wouldn't they?

On the road it had been quiet. With nothing more than the sounds of horses and voices of the men, it was peaceful. They were usually alone as their party traveled through the countryside, only occasionally passing other travelers.

Walking inside the inn was like turning the volume up so loud you could hear the song five cars away as the bass pounded through your chest. It was hot inside from all the bodies and roaring fire. Make that unwashed bodies. She wrinkled her nose and took a step back.

"Is aught amiss?"

She looked up at James.

"It's a bit overwhelming. Kind of a drastic change from the quiet of falling snow, and the horses and men."

"Your ears will become accustomed to the sounds. 'Tis not as loud as you believe."

"Welcome. 'Tis an honor to have such a fine lord in our presence." The innkeeper stood in front of them, wiping his hands on his apron. He was a rotund man with a big smile. Melinda liked him instantly.

James nodded. "We require rooms."

The innkeeper's face fell. He gestured to the room around him. "Apologies. Your men can sleep here in the main room. We've only the one room upstairs." He stood there looking miserable, wringing his hands. Melinda felt sorry for him.

"One room will do. My men and my lady require food and drink."

James led her to a large table in the back of the room. Wherever they went, she noticed he liked his back to the wall with a clear view of anyone coming or going. His men sat on the benches. Their party of seven seemed to tip the scales, filling the inn to overflowing.

Renly leaned across the table, pitching his voice low. "My

lord, I do not care for the look of those men."

Melinda noticed Renly would call James by his given name when it was just the two of them. When there were more people around, he used the formal "my lord." From what she'd gathered, they'd been fighting together for many years.

Melinda watched James. He would've made a great spy. He didn't even turn his head. And she knew instantly he had taken the temperature of the room. She bet if she asked him, he could tell her about every single person. Intrigued, she put it to the test.

"The man at the table next to the window when we came in—what color is his tunic?"

Renly looked at her funny. James leaned back against the wall.

"His hair is the color of wheat, brown tunic, and he carries a knife in each boot. Though he is in his cups and would not throw straight." The disgust in his voice made she and Renly laugh.

"I totally missed the knives."

A serving wench bustled over, flirting with the men as she made her way through the big, open room. The inn had a stone floor, and Melinda noticed there were bones scattered around, as if some of the diners couldn't be bothered to leave them on the table and simply threw them on the floor. There were several dogs throughout the room. Most of the dogs were well behaved, if in need of a bath.

The large hearth boasted a roaring fire. Melinda could see a back room where most of the cooking must take place.

The tables were wood, with long benches so you sat side by side with other diners.

Every time the door opened, a gust of cold air whooshed inside, making Melinda glad they were in the back of the room, even if it was a bit claustrophobic.

"Keep a few of the men on guard." James turned to her. "I will sleep outside your door tonight, ensure your safety."

There was no way she was letting him sleep on the cold stone floor outside her room, but she'd wait until they were upstairs to say anything. If he hadn't been injured, she still would've protested but might've given in. In her time, a man with his injuries would be in the hospital or at home resting, maybe going to physical therapy. She could tell by the way he moved that his injuries still bothered him. But this wasn't the place to have that discussion—there were too many ears around.

And Melinda was finding that medieval men and women were bigger gossips than any of the women she'd encountered at home.

The serving wench poured ale for the men. She and James drank wine. She knew he was drinking wine only because she was. Otherwise he drank ale with his men. They were a close-knit group. Trusted each other with their lives. She knew they would keep her safe.

The food finally came. Her stomach growled in anticipation. Dinner was roast chicken with bread and carrots. Melinda had never been so happy to have chicken, after all the wild boar.

They quit talking as everyone dug into the food. It was

hot and tasty, and she ate until she thought her stomach would burst.

James bade Renly and the men goodnight. "I will see the lady to her room."

His captain nodded. "Goodnight, mistress."

Melinda waved to the men. She'd grown very fond of them in the short time she'd been here. They were overly solicitous of her, making sure she rested enough. One of them would say he needed to go the bathroom or rest for a moment, and she knew it was all for her benefit. She was grateful they paid attention to her needs.

"Goodnight, all. Don't let the bedbugs bite."

A couple of the men looked at her funny, and Melinda laughed. At home they said it jokingly, but here? She better inspect the bedding. The thought of bedbugs made her skin itch.

James opened the door. "Stay here a moment."

He went inside, looked at the room, checked the window, and then nodded to her to come in. The room was small but cozy. The bed looked large enough to sleep four people. She sat down, hearing the crunch. No featherbed or nice sheets here, but it was better than the cold ground and there didn't seem to be any bugs. There was a small ewer and basin in the room for washing, and a fireplace. She went to the fire, stretching her hands toward the warmth.

"I will sleep outside the door."

"I don't think that's a good idea." She held up a hand. "Hear me out. I know you don't like anyone to mention it, but you haven't fully recovered from your injuries. If you sleep on the cold stone floor, you'll be stiff in the morning."

James stood ramrod straight, scowling. "'Tis no different than sleeping on the ground at night."

"That may be true, but I saw you limping when you got off your horse. I won't be able to sleep if I know you're outside on the floor. Don't you want me to get a good night's sleep tonight? And what if those men downstairs cause problems when we leave in the morning? You might be a moment slower because you ache from sleeping on the floor."

"It would not be proper for me to sleep in the same room."

"We have slept side by side on the ground for over a week."

"That is different."

"No, it really isn't. Just pretend we're still outside. You sleep on your side of the bed, I'll sleep on mine."

"This is an argument I will not win, is it, lady?"

Melinda put her hands on her hips. "Nope. So just be a nice, chivalrous knight and give in now."

He made her a bow. "As the lady wishes."

Melinda went over to the bed and lifted up the blanket and sheet and examined them for the second time.

"What are you doing?"

"Looking for bugs."

James looked like he was going to say something then shut his mouth. He went to the door and looked over his shoulder.

"I will have a word with the men then I'll be back. I'll

send someone to help you undress."

And he walked out the door. Talk about leaving on a loaded word. Melinda hadn't thought about being undressed in the same bed as James.

On the road they'd all slept in their clothes and wrapped in cloaks to keep warm. But here? Their clothes were pretty grungy from traveling for a week. She really didn't want to sleep in them. Would he sleep in his shirt? What if he slept in the nude? Melinda fanned her face, thinking about all that muscled skin on display.

Chapter Twenty-Two

No bath for her tonight, but at least Melinda would be able to wash. Though it wouldn't be like a hot shower and her favorite mandarin-orange-scented shower gel. She could almost conjure up the scent. The serving wench was busy with one of the men, whatever that meant. Melinda's imagination presented her with all kinds of interesting images.

The door opened and the innkeeper's wife bustled in carrying a cloth and what looked suspiciously like a misshapen snowball. The smell of lavender filled the room. The woman handed her the lump and the cloth.

"A fine lady from France paid for her lodging with these lovely soaps. I thought a lady such as yourself would enjoy it."

"Thank you. I love the scent of lavender."

The plump woman gestured to the fire. "I'll start the water." She set a bucket and basin on the floor. Seeing

Melinda's look, she said, "To wash your hair, dearie."

Melinda's hand went to the tangled mess. "I'm sure it's full of sticks and leaves from traveling."

The woman helped her undress. She shook out the dress and cloak and laid them over a chair. "I'll scrub some of the mud out. They'll dry by the fire tonight."

Melinda sat on the stool and leaned her head back. The woman poured warm water over her hair and Melinda heard it falling into the bucket. It was such a treat to have someone wash her hair. That was always her favorite part of a haircut.

The woman used the lavender soap to wash her hair. She plucked out leaves and twigs, all the while keeping up a constant stream of chatter.

Melinda reached up to wipe water from her face.

"You don't have any hair in your arm-hole."

She'd better not, with all the money she'd spent on electrolysis for her armpits and upper lip. Too bad the hair on her legs wasn't dark enough for lasers. She had to rely on waxing, which meant if she was stuck here she'd have to find out how to shave her legs.

"Where I come from, ladies remove the hair."

"'Tis a strange land." The woman crossed herself and launched into a tale about the Frenchwoman who'd stayed for several days, and her scandalous behavior.

Melinda closed her eyes, listening to the gossip. The woman knew everything about everyone in the village. And all the travelers coming and going from the inn.

"It sounds very exciting. Different people coming and

going all the time."

The woman held up a twig. "Were you rolling in the leaves, dearie?"

"I did roll down a hill once. Not watching where I was walking."

"No doubt watching the arse of that fine man yer traveling with."

She and the innkeeper's wife laughed.

"The Red Knight used to be a beautiful man." The woman sighed, rinsed Melinda's hair one last time, and stood. Melinda heard the woman dumping the bucket out of the window onto the ground.

"'Tis a shame." She winked at Melinda. "Though the dark hides scars. I'd like a tumble or two with him."

Warmth spread out over Melinda's chest and up her face. "He's very strong."

"Indeed. Shall I help you wash, lady?"

"I can wash myself. You've done more than enough."

As Melinda turned to soak her stockings in the water with a little sliver of the soap, the woman gasped.

"You don't have hair on your legs like a wee girl. But lady, the mark on your back..." The innkeeper's wife crossed herself. "I've seen similar strange markings on pagans. Are you a pagan, lady?"

"No, I'm not pagan. Where I come from, everyone has a mark. And all the ladies remove the hair from their bodies."

The innkeeper's wife looked dubious, and Melinda bet she'd be the next topic of gossip. The woman gave a short nod and backed out of the room as quickly as she could.

Melinda had forgotten about her tattoo. When she graduated from college, she did it to mark the occasion.

It was on her shoulder blade. The simple shape of the sun. To remind her no matter how far she went from home, she would always remember where she came from. The funny thing was, she never left Holden Beach. She'd always thought she would travel the world, but ended up staying in the town where she was born and raised. She had no regrets.

Though be careful what you wish for. Now it looked like she was getting her wish to see other parts of the world. Even if she did have to travel over seven hundred years to the past to do it.

Melinda wrinkled her nose. Her chemise needed a good wash, but then she wouldn't have anything to wear. The innkeeper's wife had done a good job of getting the mud and stains out of the cloak and dress. Both were damp and steaming next to the fire. She'd put the cloak back to dry before she went to bed. Right now she wrapped it around herself and sat down in a chair next to the fire. There was a knock at the door and the serving wench rushed in, looking a bit disheveled.

"Yer husband bid me bring wine. He's an ugly one."

The girl put the jug and cups on the table and left the room with a flounce, hips swaying.

Melinda wanted to slap the tart. James was not ugly. He couldn't help what had been done to him. She noticed the innkeeper and his wife also assumed they were married. It was probably best to let them go on thinking so, as they were sharing a room.

She pulled a comb out of her satchel to run through her hair. What did they use for conditioner? A couple of swearwords left her mouth just as the door opened and James strode in.

"Crap on toast."

He stood there, a smile on his face, letting her know he'd heard every word.

"Let me." He took the comb from her, pulled up the stool, and sat down behind her.

"It's all tangled. The innkeeper's wife got the leaves and twigs out, but I don't think I'll ever get the knots out. Maybe I should cut it all off."

"Patience."

Melinda snorted. "You're a fine one to talk. Before you work on my hair, let me get you a glass of wine. You're going to need it."

She stood and poured them both a glass. It was a red wine with a hint of blackberries. Melinda was becoming a fan of wine.

"You were gone a long time. Is everything all right?"

"Renly and the men will keep watch." James went to work on her hair.

The fire crackled. Voices and the clinking of crockery, the sounds of horses outside in the stable, and the warmth of the room lulled her into a state of deep relaxation. James was gentle. As he worked out each knot, he didn't tug or pull. The man had more patience in his finger than she possessed in her entire body. His fingers skimmed the back of her neck and shoulders as he brushed out each tangle.

"The innkeeper's wife also had a dress in her possession. The same French lady who left the soap left a new gown. I believe it will fit. I'm sorry there wasn't time to have a few more dresses made for you before we left."

She felt his breath on her skin, making goosebumps break out on her flesh as he spoke. A heaviness settled over the room.

"A new dress? Thank you. As much as I would like to wear something clean, I think I'll save it until we get to Blackford. I want to look nice when we arrive."

He grunted and went back to combing her hair. They sat together in companionable silence, James rhythmically brushing her hair, the curls crackling with static as they dried before the fire. Melinda caught herself jerking awake.

He put the comb down on the table and stood, reaching out a hand. She placed her hand in his, feeling the calluses on his fingers. Mere inches separated them. So close she could feel his breath on her face, smell a hint of wine. The flames from the fire reflected in his emerald eyes.

Ever so slowly, he leaned in, the tension in the room so real it was like another person standing next to her taking up all the space. A loud bang and the sound of booted feet running down the stairs made him jerk back. Melinda put her palms to her face.

He'd almost kissed her.

And she'd wanted him to.

Chapter Twenty-Three

Melinda woke in the morning to find herself curled up to James, his arm wrapped around her. She didn't move, simply looked at him. In his arms she felt safe and secure. Cherished.

She whispered, "Boy oh boy, you're in big trouble. You're falling for him. Hard."

At home everything moved faster. Dating happened at a much faster pace. Here, though, everything was slower. It was a nice change. To really get to know someone before taking things to the next level. Happiness bloomed within her. He'd almost kissed her last night. Did he feel the same?

She sat up in bed, the covers slipping from her shoulders. The chemise was modest enough. James slept in his shirt. And nothing else. She'd tried not to think about that as she'd fallen asleep last night. Maybe just a tiny peek. As she lifted the covers, he spoke. He startled her so badly, she almost fell out of bed.

"Is that a pagan mark on your shoulder?" The blasted man was looking at her as if he knew exactly what she'd been about to do.

"The innkeeper's wife asked me the same thing last night. It's not a pagan mark. It's called a tattoo. In my time, lots of people have them. Of all kinds of different things. Whatever is important to them, I guess. I have two."

When he sat up, his shirt gaped open. Melinda caught a glimpse of numerous scars running across his chest. How many other marks did he have on his body? When he climbed into bed last night, she'd sucked in a breath at all the old and new scars on his legs. The man was a warrior and had the marks to show for it.

He looked intrigued. "'Tis the sun." He reached out, tracing the tattoo, his touch like the warmth of the sun against her skin.

"What is the other mark? Where is it?"

She turned to face him, placing a hand on her left hipbone.

"The other one is here. It's a quote from one of my favorite childhood books, *Through the Looking Glass*. It says, 'Sometimes I've believed as many as six impossible things before breakfast.'"

"You have writing on your body? Why?"

Melinda had never explained the tattoo to anyone. No one blinked an eye at the beach when she wore a bikini and the writing showed. They'd become commonplace enough that no one really paid attention. And in her experience, most people were too self-absorbed to notice.

"My parents died in a boating accident when I was twelve. My aunt raised us. Losing your parents at a young age changes you."

She looked at him. "You know this. When I turned eighteen and was going off to college, I wanted something that said to me I could go on no matter what. No matter how hard things were, I would keep going. The quote from my favorite book stayed with me. I think that's why I chose it. Because if you believe in the impossible, it makes you think you can do anything." She grinned. "Like travel through time."

James touched her shoulder then ran his hands through her hair.

"Your hair is like fire." He picked up the pouch he wore around his waist and dug into it. "Hold out your hand."

He dropped a lock of hair into her palm.

"How did you get this?"

"The day you arrived on my lands and almost lost your pretty head."

"The sword cut that close?"

"Aye. I picked it up off the ground and have been carrying it around ever since as a knight treasures a token from his lady."

Her hand went to her hair. It was so thick she'd never noticed.

He grabbed a fistful of hair and pulled her to him. Melinda didn't know why she expected the kiss to be gentle. It wasn't. It was a warrior's kiss, and she felt it all the way to her toes. When he pulled away, she felt adrift at sea.

With one kiss he'd obliterated every other kiss she'd ever had. It was like a new beginning, a first kiss. She put a finger to her lips. A look of pure male satisfaction filled James' face.

And then...the spell surrounding them broke. Melinda didn't know what had changed, only that James turned away, frowning. He yanked his clothes on, angry for no reason.

She made a show of gathering her clothes. When she turned around, he was dressed.

"I'll send someone to help you dress, lady."

Oh. So they were back to lady again. What on earth had she done? Truth rocked her to the core. He believed himself to be a beast. That no one could care for him. He was like one of those women who wouldn't accept getting older and had so much plastic surgery they ended up looking like an alien. The stubborn idiot wouldn't believe she cared for him.

Melinda couldn't make him see himself through her eyes. He would have to get past his injuries or hide in the shadows for the rest of his life. She was done with trying to change a man. If he wouldn't let her in, she would let go, find Lucy, and go back home to the life she'd left behind. And forget all about her grumpy knight...

Chapter Twenty-Four

James cursed. Why had he kissed Melinda? The man he was before his injuries would've kissed her without a second thought. But now—she was polite not to pull away in disgust. Did she regret the kiss?

For he knew—he'd visited every eligible noble maiden in the realm, and all ran screaming from him or fainted. Women no longer found him pleasing. All his gold would not entice a woman to gaze upon his visage for the rest of her life. James was kissing her, letting her know with one kiss how much he cared. How afraid he was he'd lose her. And then he knew...he cared for this woman claiming to be from the future. Then he caught his reflection in the basin of water. Saw the beast.

He pulled away, shattering the moment between them. Ever since he woke, he'd been in a foul humor. Grunted at his men and ignored Melinda. How dare the sun shine? Rain would agree with his black mood. They traveled a good distance before stopping for lunch. He'd purchased food from the innkeeper to bring with them on the journey. As they ate and the horses grazed, Melinda brushed her hands off on her dress. She spoke to Renly, not meeting his gaze. She could not bear to look at him.

"I saw a stream nearby. I want to wash the mud off the bottom of my clothes."

His captain looked to him. James nodded grimly.

"As you wish, lady."

During their travel they had not encountered any other travelers. James did not send a guard with her. He sat on a flat rock in the sun and brooded. Feeling sorry for himself.

Melinda wanted to smack James. He'd been cranky all morning. If he regretted the kiss, he should just say so instead of stomping around. She wanted to ask him, but didn't want the men to hear. She'd wait until tonight, find a moment to pull him aside and ask him what his problem was.

The cold water soothed her temper. There was grease on her hands from lunch. She rubbed them with mud from the bank. Once her hands were clean, Melinda squatted down to wet the hem of her cloak and dress in the stream. She sat on a rock and scrubbed the cloth against the stone, repeating until the clothing was as clean as she could manage with water. Since she would be wearing the same clothes for the rest of the way, she wanted to stay as clean as possible. She'd never gone without deodorant at home. With a quick look around to make sure she was alone, Melinda sniffed her pits. Thanks to daily scrubs with water and the rest of the precious lavender soap, she didn't stink. The new dress would wait until they arrived at Blackford. She didn't want Lucy to see her looking like something the cat dragged out of the trash.

Movement caught her eye. There. Across the shallow stream was the most adorable bunny sitting there looking at her. It was brown and plump, with the cutest pink nose. As it turned to hop away, Melinda followed. She knew she had a bit of time. The men would let the horses eat while they finished their meal.

There were large trees on the right, and on the left shrubbery along the base of the trees. So it would be easy to mark her path. No way she'd get lost, and she wouldn't go far. The bunny hopped around a corner and Melinda picked up her pace, following along until she came out of the trees into a meadow.

Magical. As if she'd tumbled down the rabbit hole and landed in the land of faeries.

The meadow was filled with crocus and bluebells. The first signs of life after winter. The sun turned the meadow into an impressionist painting. There was a grouping of stones almost in the center of the meadow. She made her way there, climbed up, and stretched out on the flat stone, letting the sun warm her. Just a few minutes.

Melinda opened her eyes. The sun had moved across the sky. Crap on toast. She'd fallen asleep. But for how long? James was going to kill her. They'd be worried and looking for her.

On the way back, things looked different. The big trees were on the left, but after several hundred yards nothing looked familiar. She retraced her steps and this time turned right.

"Hell's bells." Great. She was hopelessly lost. Why hadn't she tied her hair ribbons to branches? Because she'd been sure she could find her way. That was Melinda's problem— she was always sure which way to go.

Once she and a friend got turned around on vacation in the mountains of Asheville. Her friend, knowing about the Merriweather curse, asked Melinda which way to go. She said right. Three hours later, they realized if they'd turned left they would have been back at the hotel in minutes. When her friend complained, Melinda said, "You know how bad I am with directions." "Yes," the friend replied, "but you sounded so sure."

Who knew how long she wandered? She looked at the sky. Maybe late afternoon? She could picture the frowns from the men. They would be angry, and she didn't blame them. It was stupid to go off alone. In the future she'd better take one of the men along, no matter where she went, so she didn't get lost again. A branch snapped, making her jump. It wasn't wise to be alone in the woods. That was a lesson she'd learned the hard way.

Another noise. She scrambled over a fallen tree, digging

out the leaves to make a hiding spot when she heard someone clearing their throat.

"What, pray tell, are you about, mistress?"

Melinda popped up.

"Renly. I'm so glad it's you."

She held her hands out in a placating gesture.

"I'm so sorry. I got lost again. Don't say it—I should've taken one of the men with me. But when I was at the stream, I saw a bunny and followed him. To the most magical place. Come see."

Apparently she'd gone in a circle, because Melinda could see the meadow beyond the break in the trees. Renly silently stood beside her. James' captain took a medallion out of his tunic, kissed it, and walked into the center of the meadow, touching the stones. The expression of awe on his face probably mirrored her own.

"'Tis a sacred place."

They stood quietly, enjoying the feeling of peace in the air.

"We needs return. Lord Falconburg will be worried."

She snorted. "More like furious."

"He will understand. 'Tis in your nature."

"My nature?"

"You were given great beauty but no sense of direction."

Melinda ignored him. He led her back through the woods, across the stream, and back to the camp.

"How do you do that?" He looked at her, a question on his face. Before he could answer, she spoke again. "How do you walk so quietly and find your way so easily?"

Renly looked perplexed. "I would ask the same of you, lady. How do you sound like a herd or horses and end up lost no matter where we travel?"

"It's a gift to make perfect men like you feel needed."

He threw back his head and laughed. As they walked into the camp, he quit laughing, his hand going to the sword at his hip. He unsheathed the blade, shoving Melinda behind him with his free hand.

"What?"

She peered around him and clapped a hand over her mouth. One of the men, the youngest one with red hair, lay on the ground, eyes open and unseeing. Two more of the men sat on the ground, blood on their tunics. Another came stumbling from the woods at the opposite side of the camp.

"We were attacked. Never heard them. I was taking a piss when I heard a commotion. I chased after them but it was too late." The man held out his sword to Renly.

"Kill me, captain. For I have failed. The men took Lord Falconburg."

Renly and Melinda swore at the same time. This was all her fault. If she hadn't followed the bunny or spent so much time in the meadow, then gotten lost, they would've been on their way and been long gone before the men came. Now a man was dead because of her.

"We will camp in the meadow. The spirits will keep us safe. Bring Ben. We will bury him there. It will be dark soon. We cannot search for James tonight. In the morning, we will find him. I swear it, my lady."

One of the injured men saw to the horses. Both had

suffered cuts and bruises, but nothing fatal. Renly and the other two men carried Ben. At the meadow, Melinda stayed with the horses as they buried the fallen knight. She stood side by side with them around the grave. No one knew what to say, so she recited a prayer she remembered from childhood.

How many times had James come to her rescue since she'd arrived in medieval England?

Now it was her turn to save him.

Chapter Twenty-Five

"Bloody hell. I'll go find her." The irksome wench had no sense of direction. Small babes could find their way home easier than Melinda. James never got lost.

He tracked her through the forest to the stream. The print of her boot told him she'd crossed it. He followed the tracks through the wood. A broken branch showed him her path. There were tracks of a hare. Why would she follow the animal? She couldn't bear to watch them kill the food the men caught.

Something in the brush glittered in the light. One of Melinda's earrings. As James bent down to pick up the jewelry, cold steel met his neck. The blade lifted, forcing him to his feet if he didn't want to lose his head. His leg trembled but didn't fail.

"What have we here? The Red Knight caught off his guard."

A group of outlaws surrounded him. James met the gaze

of the man who held the blade to his neck. He knew who they were. They lived in a dark wood, preyed on travelers and held nobles and knights for ransom. 'Twas rumored they were led by a man who was once a rich and powerful knight. No one knew who he was.

James whirled away from the blade, pulling the man toward him. He struck the dolt, gratified to hear the breath whoosh out. The masked outlaw kicked his leg out and James went down hard, taking his opponent with him. He rolled to his feet, striking the whoreson. As the man raised his knife, James leaned in, feeling the cut of steel on his arm as he removed the bandit's mask.

He was so taken aback by the man's face that James missed the fist coming straight for his nose. A loud crunch followed by pain, gushing blood, and the taste of warm metal filling his mouth all told James his nose was broken. Again.

The man leaned down, picked up the mask, dusted it off on his hose, and shrugged.

James gaped at him. "Your brothers think you dead."

"Everyone thinks I'm dead. I intend to keep it that way."

The man before him was renowned. One of five brothers, John Thornton was the second son. According to rumor, he had been caught in bed with the king's mistress. John escaped death but lost all. His title, lands, and money. The rest of his family suffered heavy fines. Some lost lands and title. But over the years, serving as mercenaries and fighting in tourneys, they regained their wealth and status.

The man offered his hand. "Mayhap you would care to

wear a mask as well?"

James grunted, slapped John's hand away, and got to his feet. He wobbled but a moment before standing steady. He would not show weakness in front of this man. No matter how his body pained him.

"Why not tell your brothers you live?"

"My death keeps them safe. The price on my head is too high. And I will never be welcome at court again. I ask you to keep my secret."

"You ask a great deal."

"I live in these woods. Ransoming knights and nobles. Killing many. I could kill you as well."

James scoffed. "Ransom would be more profitable than killing me. You know I am wealthy."

"Some say more so than the king. You will keep my secret."

"Pray tell."

All the Thornton brothers were arrogant whoresons. James had fought against all of them during battles and tourneys. A fearsome bunch of warriors, and while he would never admit such to the man before him, James respected them, even though they were cousin to his most hated enemy.

"I know why you hate William Brandon. But your hatred is in vain. I will tell the truth in return for my secret."

James knew the story of his family's massacre. What could this man know James did not? Curiosity filling him, he extended a hand.

"We have an accord."

John shook his hand. "Not so pretty anymore, are you?" He pointed at James' face. "Who did that to you?"

James' leg was trembling, and he knew it would not be long before he found himself on the ground writhing in pain. "'Tis best a tale heard over a drink."

John Thornton chuckled. "Where are my manners? And James?"

A raven cawed above them. As it flew from the tree, a single black feather floated down, landing next to James' foot.

John nodded to his men.

"I'm sorry."

"For what?

Pain exploded in James' head.

James woke to find himself blindfolded and trussed up like a wild boar, his hands and feet tied to branches as John's men carried him through the woods. The scent of cooking fires and sounds of people told him they were close to the outlaw's home. The men dropped him on the ground. One of the men removed the ropes binding his hands and feet.

James rubbed his hands and feet while he sat on the ground looking around him, noting any weakness. From the looks of the place, John had been living here for many years.

'Twas a small village built deep within the wood. Small wooden homes with children playing, women coming and going, and many men.

Many stared at him curiously, but not a single person shrieked or ran away in fear. Mayhap they were used to beasts. 'Twas said the wood was haunted by evil spirits.

One of the men led him to a wooden home larger than the others. The inside was well appointed. Rugs on the floors, fine furniture, and tapestries on the wall. No doubt stolen goods.

John handed him a mug of ale.

"My apologies for dealing you a blow. Our location must be kept secret. 'Tis safer for all that way."

They sat drinking as a woman entered bearing a platter of food. James' stomach growled. He couldn't remember the last time he'd eaten. No doubt his men would be searching for him. He hoped they'd found Melinda unharmed. The vexing woman found herself in more trouble than a small, curious boy.

"The last time I saw you as a lad, you had a pretty face and all the maids swooned at your feet."

James grimaced, touching the scar at his eye.

"'Twas the Boltons from the south. Sir Bolton was offended I would not marry his daughter. The man tried to deceive me. The blacksmith got her with child."

James discreetly picked a small rock out of his bread.

"Before he would have paid me to make his daughter Lady Falconburg. Now he would not have me to wed for all my gold and lands. Said I would produce deformed offspring. No man could have survived such wounds. Therefore I must be demon."

"I always knew you were a demon." John chuckled and raised a glass.

Chapter Twenty-Six

James wiped his mouth on his sleeve.

"What do you know of my family's massacre?"

John Thornton, outlaw of the wood, stretched his legs out in front of him.

"Your father's steward lied. Clement Grey promised the man a great deal of gold for lying. Clement was William's half-brother, though William never knew until the end. Clement wanted William dead for many years. Jealousy will twist a man into a deformed creature. Now he is dead by William's own hand."

"The Greys were a loathsome family."

"Aye. My words are true: William did kill your brother in battle. But not in a cowardly manner. 'Twas a fair fight."

John gazed into the fire as he told the tale. James gripped the arms of the chair so hard the tendons in his hands stood out. He forced himself to ease his grip. To show no weakness.

"I was there. A page to a most ferocious night. I was eleven years old."

James forced himself to remain calm.

"And my brother, Henry?"

"He was at the battle but did not see the fight between William and your eldest brother."

"What of the massacre? William and his men were there. Killed them all. The servants talk of the story to this day."

John rested his elbows on his knees.

"William was lured there by a messenger. He thought a woman was in danger, held against her will. 'Twas a lie. Clement always coveted what William had. He tried to kill the woman William later married. In truth, Clement and Georgina hired mercenaries to kill your family. The two of them plotted, thinking your family would retaliate, killing William for them."

James kept his gaze focused on John's face, looking for any sign the man was lying. He could find none.

"Finish the tale."

"William never knew Georgina and Clement plotted against him. He would not listen to the truth. Then 'twas too late. Georgina died. Rumor was he killed her. But William did not kill Georgina. The rumors persisted, even through the first years of his marriage to Lady Blackford. As to your family, the servants didn't see William until the end. He came upon the mercenaries killing your family and killed as many as he could. Bloodied from battle, the servants found him leaning over your mother's body. He was trying to save her, not kill her. He tracked down the few mercenaries who escaped, and killed them."

James found the story difficult to believe. His entire life, he'd grown up hearing the story his father's steward told. Hearing the truth was difficult, even as John's words carried the ring of truth.

"What is Lady Blackford's given name?"

John raised a brow, a speculative look in his eye.

"She is a strange one. The servants are loyal to her; none will speak against her. I believe her name is Lucy Merriweather. Do you know the lady?"

Melinda was right. The lady and her sister were the same person.

"Will you write down what you have told me? Swear to it?"

John shook his head.

"I cannot. Such a letter would expose me."

James had been wrong his entire life. Hated a man he had no cause to hate.

"Why did William never tell me the truth?"

"You were told this story by your father's trusted steward. Told the same story since you were a babe by all the servants. Would you have believed him? Your family's mortal enemy?"

"No." James shook his head slowly. He would not have believed the man. Would have cut him down where he stood.

"I didn't think so. Now we are even. Though I still plan to ransom you."

John poured another mug of ale for both of them.

"Or mayhap I should kill you. Ensure my secret stays safe."

A woman entered the room. "The herbs you asked for."

John nodded. The woman sprinkled the foul-smelling herbs into a mug and poured hot water over them. She handed the mug to James.

"She is a powerful healer. Drink the brew. Your injuries will heal." Then John grinned at him. "But you will have to live with that face. She cannot remove scars."

The woman handed him the mug. James sniffed. It smelled terrible. He took a breath and choked down the drink.

"Bloody hell, it tastes terrible."

She touched the scars on his face.

"Without these scars you would not have met the woman who is fated for you. Another would've taken her place were your visage unblemished."

"Who is this woman?"

Could she mean Melinda?

"She's the woman who will save you, Red Knight. See you for the man you were meant to be."

The healer patted his shoulder. "Sprinkle the herbs into your drink morning and night for a fortnight."

Chapter Twenty-Seven

Melinda woke to the sound of the men moving about.

"Don't y'all leave without me."

"You should remain here, lady."

"If you think I'm staying here while you go and look for James, you're out of your ever-loving mind."

Melinda put her hands on her hips, glaring at Renly and the rest of James' men.

The captain of the guard threw up his hands.

"As the lady wishes. You must try not to make noise or talk."

Melinda followed the good captain and his men into the forest. She didn't have a clue how they could figure out where to go, but one of James' men was supposed to be able to track anyone or anything.

The men were ballerinas and she was a hippo wearing a tutu. That was what she felt like as the men glided through the woods. No matter where Melinda stepped, a branch cracked or something rustled. She really did try to be quiet, but every step made her sound like a herd of small children as they made their way deeper into the wood. Heck, forget a herd of kids—she made enough noise for an entire army.

Talk about creepy. With every step, she felt as if something or someone was watching. She'd always laughed at the expression "the woods have eyes"...never again.

Stepping over a branch, Melinda wished she'd worn her old clothes. The dark green dress was beautiful, made her feel like she belonged, but it was terrible for traveling. Getting on and off a horse, hiking, and walking through the wood, it was totally impractical.

The tracker looked to be about her size. Maybe she could swipe a pair of his hose. They were kind of like leggings.

The smell of a wood-burning fire wafted through the trees. She inhaled deeply. Melinda loved that smell. It reminded her of cold nights, hot chocolate, and staying up all night with her sisters talking and laughing.

The sound of voices carried through the wood. The men stopped, listening. They started to fan out while she stayed behind Renly.

"Stay close to me. James will take my head if you are hurt."

"Consider me glued to you." She had every intention of staying close. The woods spooked her. Who knew what they were walking into?

The trees gave way to a clearing and what looked like a tiny village plopped down in the middle of the forest. Straight out of a fairytale. If she saw a cottage made of candy, she was out of here. The witch wouldn't eat James. He was all muscle and sinew, but she had a bit of plumpness. Great. Now she thought fairytales were real. *You time-traveled. Why can't fairytales be real?* The voice in her head was so not helping.

She heard the clear sound of steel ringing across the trees. Renly unsheathed his sword and chaos erupted. There was a sword propped against a tree looking lonely. Melinda picked it up with a grunt and slung it up on her shoulder just like she'd seen James do so many times.

"Yikes. These things are heavier than they look."

Renly put a hand to his mouth.

"Don't you dare laugh."

He coughed and turned his back for a moment, shoulders shaking. She narrowed her eyes. He was laughing. Before she could fuss at him, a man appeared.

"Renly, look. It's Robin Hood."

"Nay, lady. 'Tis the leader of the outlaws."

Well, he was wearing a mask and had blond hair. Didn't Robin Hood have blond hair?

The leader jerked his head and James walked forward, a man on either side of him. He wasn't tied up, but by the number of swords out and ready, she had no doubt he was being held against his will.

Before Renly spoke, Melinda brandished the sword in front of her, prayed her arms wouldn't fall off, and stepped forward.

"Let him go or I will run you through."

The man looked at her for a full count of ten. She knew.

She counted. Instead of killing her, he threw back his head and laughed. Laughed until he doubled over. It wasn't that funny. She could stick him with the sword. She eyed the end. It looked sharp enough to do damage.

His men laughed with him, which only made her madder. Had she said the wrong thing? No, "run you through" was what she'd heard the men say before they did away with bandits.

She imagined a string pulling her head to the sky, making her stand up straight.

"I will not ask you again, sir. Release Lord Falconburg now."

Chapter Twenty-Eight

Mr. Hollywood made a motion, and all at once his men lowered their swords. Melinda nodded at Renly, who looked to James then to the men.

"Put your swords away for now, lads. They may see use yet," Renly said.

"Are you all right? Did they hurt you?"

James looked stunned. Hadn't anyone ever asked him how he was after a fight? It made Melinda sad.

"I am well, my lady."

She saw the corner of his mouth twitch. He was happy to see her, or thought she looked ridiculous leaning on a sword. She'd go with happy to see her.

The masked man stepped forward, making her an exaggerated bow.

"Who is this vision of loveliness?"

Melinda heard James make some kind of growly sound as she rolled her eyes. She no longer cared for men spouting flowery compliments. No, she liked a certain grumpy knight who, when he smiled, lit up the entire room. When she looked at James, he was wearing his "I am a warrior" look. Renly stepped forward so she could step behind him if trouble broke out.

"We are here to negotiate the release of Lord Falconburg." He looked to Melinda and nodded. "Allow me to present Lady Merriweather."

"You may call me John."

The man looked her over. She saw lively brown eyes through the mask. He had blond hair down to his shoulders. There were many women back in Holden Beach who paid lots of money every month for hair like his. He looked like some kind of movie star playing at being Robin Hood in the woods. And before she met James, she would've been all about a guy as good-looking as him.

Not now. Now she liked a certain man who wore his scars on the outside. Everyone bore scars. Who cared if they showed?

"What will you trade, lady?"

"Trade?"

John sat down on a wooden bench. Everyone else followed his lead. So, she was to negotiate for James' release. Fine. Mr. Hollywood was about to find out just how good she was at negotiating.

As she walked to sit across from the man, she whispered to Renly, "I've got this."

He inclined his head. "As you wish."

Before sitting down, Melinda made a show of walking

around James, looking him over.

"Have you damaged him in any way? I expect to get him back in the same condition as when he left."

"He is better, lady. My healer has given him herbs to heal his injuries. He is now more valuable."

They went back and forth, discussing James as if he were a nice piece of antique furniture. She made sure to keep her most skeptical look plastered on her face. She peeked at James out of the corner of her eye. He seemed to be amused. Time to wrap this up and get back on the road.

"I suppose you usually accept gold?"

"Gold will suffice."

Melinda lifted her necklace out from under the dress, pulled it over her head, and held it up to the light. The gems sparkled. She knew that look. He wanted the necklace.

"The necklace is made of gold. There is an emerald, a diamond, a sapphire, and a gold charm in the form of the unicorn. Unicorns are powerful. The necklace has been blessed and will bring the wearer great fortune and luck."

She crossed her fingers behind her back. Technically it had been blessed. Aunt Pittypat wore it when she attended mass over Easter in St. Peter's Square several years ago. The Pope gave his blessing, so the necklace was blessed. As to bringing good fortune... Well, it had brought her back to the past to find Lucy and meet James, hadn't it? She thought a little white lie wouldn't hurt in this particular situation.

John held out his hand.

"May I see the necklace?"

She handed him the only thing she had left of Aunt

Pittypat. As he examined the necklace, she looked around the camp. Looked like the Robin Hood myth was still going strong. The women and children looked happy. Everyone had a task. And while it was probably a hard life, not to mention a dangerous one robbing and ransoming people, Melinda thought everyone acted like they were content.

She made sure not to pay too much attention to James. After all, you weren't supposed to show too much interest in the item you wanted. A woman wearing a purple cloak came forward. Her long silver hair was braided down her back. And while her face was full of wrinkles, her eyes were full of intelligence. She held out a hand.

"Let me examine this charmed necklace."

John handed it over without hesitation. He saw her looking at the woman.

"My healer. She helped Lord Falconburg."

The woman examined the necklace, murmuring and talking softly to herself. She looked at Melinda with a shrewd eye.

"You have traveled a great distance."

Melinda snorted. What was next? For her to meet someone tall, dark, and handsome? A giggle escaped. For she had met tall, dark, and handsome. He was the captive whose release she was working to secure.

The woman touched each gem and charm, holding them in her palm. She handed the necklace back to the masked man.

"The lady does not lie. The piece is powerful."

Good. Maybe she could get James and get out of here.

The sooner they left, the sooner they could be on their way to Blackford.

"I will accept the necklace in trade...only if you, and you alone, carry Lord Falconburg out of my wood."

Chapter Twenty-Nine

Melinda's jaw dropped. She started to argue then shut her mouth. She could do this. She'd carried her sisters piggyback numerous times. Of course, he was a lot bigger and probably weighed a hundred pounds more than them. But she would do it.

She held out a hand.

"I have your word? If I carry Lord Falconburg out of here, you will allow us and his men to go free? No one will bother us?"

The man looked amused. "I give you my word." John grinned, taking her hand in his. "'Twill be a sight to see. We have an accord."

"Yes, we have an accord."

Melinda walked over to James and looked him up and down. She turned around and bent down, knees spread apart.

"Put your arms around my neck."

She could feel the anger rolling off James.

"Not now," she whispered. "Wait until we're out of here."

He wrapped his arms around her neck, the tension rolling off him.

Melinda reached behind her, pulling her arms under his legs and clasping her hands together. She slowly straightened, hoping she wouldn't fall over. He'd never forgive her. Melinda wobbled back and forth, afraid she was going to drop him. But she found her center and stood. Well, sort of.

"What have you been eating? Rocks? You weigh as much as an elephant."

John and his men laughed. Renly looked like he wanted to join in, but knew if he did he would face James in the lists later.

James whispered in her ear, "Kill me now."

"Whatever. Look at all the gold I saved you."

"Your necklace. 'Twas valuable?"

Melinda limped out of the clearing, focusing on taking one small step after another. She panted, her knees and legs shaking. *Hold it together. A little longer and you'll be safe.* They were almost out of the camp and to safety.

"The necklace belonged to my aunt. She died the day Lucy went missing. It was all I had left of her."

"I am sorry. You should not give it up. Put me down. We will find another way."

"No. Aunt Pittypat would think it exciting and romantic for Robin Hood to wear her necklace."

James scoffed. "He is not Robin Hood."

"Perhaps not. Think of what a great story we have to tell. Living in the woods with outlaws. Ransomed for a charmed talisman. Very romantic."

Melinda swore she could feel James rolling his eyes.

"You read too many of these romance books you tell me about. I am grateful."

She wanted to laugh but didn't have any extra breath to spare. Renly and the other knights followed behind. At least, she thought it was them. She couldn't risk looking back. Melinda was afraid she'd topple over if she didn't keep going, one foot in front of the other. *Breathe.*

They were almost to the edge of the wood when John called out.

"You win, lady. 'Tis too late to travel. Stay with us tonight. You have my word: no harm will come to you, Lord Falconburg, or his men."

Melinda let James down and stumbled. He caught her.

"Thank you. I think you're made of solid steel."

"Perhaps."

She'd love to soak in a hot tub for about an hour.

James called out, "We accept your hospitality."

John clapped his hands. "Let us feast, drink, and dance."

Chapter Thirty

What a dolt. James should be rescuing Melinda. She should not be rescuing him. He knew his pride was bruised. James stomped over to the large bonfire.

Someone handed him a mug of ale. Music started playing and people began to dance.

Melinda was dancing with John. James should be glad it didn't cost him any of his gold for his ransom. But he couldn't seem to get over the fact a mere woman had saved him.

He was thinking dark thoughts when she came over, out of breath.

"Will you dance with me?"

He started to grumble. She held up a hand.

"Get over yourself. I didn't pout when you saved me. And how dumb do you think I felt? I don't even know which way is north."

"I am a man. A warrior. A knight. It is my duty to rescue

you," he said stiffly.

The wench had the cheek to roll her eyes at him.

"Do you think the damsel in distress likes being in distress?" She poked him in the chest. "No. She doesn't. She feels like an idiot."

And that was all it took. His foul mood left on the wind and he smiled. With the light from the fire turning her hair to burnished copper, the curls looked alive. Her cheeks were pink from dancing. She was the most beautiful woman James had ever seen. He reached out, grabbed her around the waist, and pulled her close to him, kissing her senseless. His unease vanished when her arms came around his neck and she kissed him back.

"I am in your debt. Do you still wish to dance, lady?"

She nodded and he pulled her into the ring of dancers. Here, he did not have to worry about his scars. And as the night turned to full dark, James felt like his old self. He laughed, danced, smiled, and kissed his woman. Repeatedly.

Melinda was his. He loved her with a passion that astonished him. He only prayed she would care enough for him to be willing to marry him. He didn't expect her to love him, not the way he looked. If she would but tolerate him, it would be enough.

The next morning, they were ready to leave.

"I will talk with John, buy your necklace back."

"No. He might make me give you back."

She kissed him on the cheek. And it seemed the magic from the night before was still among them.

"I have never been rescued by a woman before. You are as brave as any of my knights."

"I've never rescued anyone. It is a very powerful feeling."

He followed her gaze. John walked around the camp, wearing the necklace.

"I know Aunt Pittypat is looking down from heaven, giggling. The thought of an infamous outlaw wearing her necklace, believing it to have magical powers. She must be laughing her head off right now."

Renly appeared before him. "The horses are ready."

They said their goodbyes. John kissed Melinda on the cheek.

"'Twas a pleasure to meet you, lady."

She smiled up at the bandit.

"No offense, but I'm just as happy to be leaving."

John laughed, the sound ringing through the wood as they rode out.

James didn't know how he had forgotten to tell her. The kissing had distracted him.

"I'm sorry I didn't tell you last night. The things John told me were difficult to hear. It seems I have been wrong my entire life."

Melinda turned in her saddle to look at him.

"What are you talking about?"

"William did not murder my family. I will tell you the tale, but you'll want to hear what else I learned." He hoped Melinda would not want to stay with her sister in Blackford. For he wanted to make her his own.

"Lady Blackford is Lucy Merriweather."

He didn't get to say another word. Melinda let out a yell. Raised her fist to the air and shook it.

"I can't believe I did it! I traveled through time to the right time and now I'll see Lucy."

She urged her horse close to his, leaned across the saddle, and tugged on his arm. He leaned toward her and she kissed him. James ignored the teasing and taunts from his men.

"Tell me everything."

As they rode, James told her what he learned from John Thornton. Told her how wrong he was about William. The lies he grew up believing. And how her sister was at Blackford.

"Are you going to talk to William? Do you think he'll listen?"

"I do not know. If it were me, I would fight first then talk."

One of Melinda's curls escaped from the ribbon where she'd tied her hair back. James wanted to reach out and take it between his hands. But he had endured enough teasing today from his men.

"If he is holding my sister against her will, I will run him through."

James smiled at her, feeling the laugh deep within his

belly as it spilled forth.

"He would be wise to fear you, my lady. You are very ferocious."

Chapter Thirty-One

The closer they got to Blackford, the more Melinda's nerves stretched tight until she thought she would snap back like a rubber band. Finally. She'd see her sister. Find out what happened. Every moment in the past, every experience, had brought her to this moment.

As they came around the bend of what passed for a road, Melinda let out a gasp. Blackford Castle. Last time she saw the castle, the entire place was a ruin. Now it stood in all its glory. Talk about impressive. Melinda cast a critical eye over the castle. Falconburg was bigger and more forbidding. Though Blackford certainly came in a close second.

Looking at the castle made her think of its owner. Could Lucy be here with William of her own free will? Melinda hadn't thought that far ahead. She'd only thought of finding Lucy and going home.

But now things were different. She wanted to be with James. And James lived on the opposite coast. In her own time it wouldn't be a big deal, she'd drive to see her sister, but here? It was a big undertaking to travel back and forth. All the Merriweather sisters made time for each other. They'd never been this far apart. Sure, Charlotte went on her trips, but it wasn't permanent.

She looked at James. He'd found out news that rocked his world, but it didn't mean he'd be up for being friends with William.

What would she do? Would she stay in the past with Lucy? Go back to Falconburg with James? Or would she travel back to her own time and make sure Charlotte was okay?

So many decisions, and none of them easy.

The closer they rode to the castle, the more Melinda's nerves pulled everything inside her tight. It was surreal to be here. Seeing the castle as a working home, not a ruin. The place in her time where her sister was presumed dead.

A man met them in the courtyard. James dismounted, throwing the reins to him.

"See to the horses. Where is Lord Blackford?"

"My lord is visiting his cousin and will return on the morrow. Lady Blackford is here. I will inform her of your arrival."

Melinda fidgeted, her breath coming in short little pants.

She couldn't believe she was actually here. James squeezed her shoulder.

"Easy. Do not worry."

The tone of his voice, the touch of his hand, calmed her enough that she could breathe normally. The doors to the great hall opened and a woman stepped out. Melinda couldn't move.

The woman was about the right height, but even from here Melinda could see her hair was silver. Her heart sank.

John was wrong. It wasn't Lucy. Her vision blurred, and something wet dripped down her face, landing on her hand with a splat. Dejected, Melinda turned away.

"Mellie!"

Melinda spun around. No one else called her Mellie. She ran. Lucy threw her arms around her.

"It is you, Mellie. How on earth did you manage to get back? Did you find my letter?"

Lucy cried. Melinda cried so hard she could hardly get the words out.

"What happened to your hair?"

Melinda touched the silvery strands, really looked at her sister. Lucy had aged. And not just a couple of years. She looked a lot older. Old enough to be their mother. Things started to go dark around the edge of her vision, the dark taking over, Lucy growing smaller and smaller until she was nothing more than a tiny pinprick.

"What happened?" She was sitting on the ground, her head resting against James' chest.

Lucy squatted down beside her. "You fainted, Mellie."

James ran his fingers through her hair. "You had quite a fright."

"Bring her inside. Your men will find food and drink in the kitchens." Lucy looked back and forth between them, a slow smile spreading across her face.

"So that's how it is. You might as well join us..."

James bowed. "James Rivers. Lord Falconburg."

Lucy looked to Melinda. "Oh, dear. I think we have a lot to talk about."

"Boy, you're not kidding."

Chapter Thirty-Two

Lady Blackford insisted they eat first. James looked around the lady's solar. It was colorful and soft. The two sisters had not stopped talking since clapping eyes on each other.

"Your letter fell apart, Lucy. You should've tried to protect it better. When I found it and opened it, the paper crumbled to dust. The only word I could make out was *safe*. And I recognized your handwriting. You always put a smiley face in the bottom of the S."

Lucy took her hands. "I'm so sorry. I thought it would last. Salt air destroys almost everything. I should have known better."

James thought Melinda and her sister had forgotten he was there. He sat back, watching them together. The moment Lucy knew her sister was the moment he knew her story was true. Both sisters had traveled through time. More than seven hundred years.

James kept looking between the two sisters, listening to

the strange words. The way they spoke. Hearing them talk, he realized how Melinda must have thought about her words before she spoke. He did not understand some of the words, but followed the conversation, understanding the meaning.

"So you actually married Simon? That jerk tricked you. Well, you aren't married now. I mean in the future. Crap on toast. In 2016."

Lucy put down the small pastry she was nibbling.

"What do you mean?"

"The church and all the records were burned to ash. Apparently the old priest kept everything on paper. He hadn't computerized anything. It was supposed to be his project for the next year. So there's no record of your marriage."

"Who owns the castle? Is it still a ruin?"

"It is, and get this."

Melinda paused. James found himself leaning forward, wanting to know what she would say.

"The Grey family never owned Blackford. The Brandon family owned the castle. The last Lord Blackford died in the fifteen hundreds. He was named Winston Brandon...let me think...some old guy said it was 1564. Winston was the last Brandon. The castle went to the National Trust."

"Winston. After Dad?"

Lucy looked as if she might faint. James set his cup on the table in case he needed to catch her. He touched his leg. The herbs the healer gave him were working. His leg still ached and trembled, but not as much.

Melinda nodded. "I know, right?"

James was glad this Simon was dead. For if he wasn't, James would've killed him. To trick a woman into marriage was a cowardly deed.

Lucy told Melinda about a curse.

"So Simon said I was Lucy Brandon. Which at the time didn't make a lick of sense. But I am Lucy Brandon...now." Lucy shook her head. "I know. It doesn't make sense. I don't know how it's possible, only that it is. Maybe you get a new life when you go back in time? I thought and thought about it, but it just makes my head hurt trying to figure it out."

Melinda leaned forward in the chair.

"So where is this husband of yours? I'm dying to meet him."

Lucy glanced over at James. "He's visiting his cousin, Edward Thornton. He should be back tomorrow. You must stay. I can't believe you traveled all the way from Falconburg in this weather. How long did it take?"

"It's a long story. I'll tell you all about it later. Let's just say it took us a few weeks to get here and it was a very eventful journey."

James looked at Melinda, saw the question in her eyes, and nodded. "We'll stay."

Melinda smiled at him. She looked so happy he wanted to pull her in his arms. Tell her how much he cared for her.

A servant brought more food and drink. James had to allow that the food was very good. The "sandwich" Melinda had created was also something her sister knew of. James took a bite and chewed. He lifted the bread to see what was inside. Content to let the sisters talk and learn more about the woman he cared for, James took another bite.

"So what year did you come through?"

Chapter Thirty-Three

Lucy touched her hair.

"1307. Twenty years ago. Gosh, I can't believe it's been twenty years. What year was it when you left?"

"2016. I planned to leave sooner, but the man Simon hired tried to kill me."

"No! He said both of you were dead. You don't know how many years I agonized over it. Felt responsible."

Melinda hugged Lady Blackford.

"You are not responsible for what that evil man did. He was already dead, but the wackjob English guy he hired—"

She looked at James. "Sorry. I don't mean all Englishmen are crazy, just a few of them."

He shrugged. "Evil finds a home when men invite it in."

One of the copper curls had come loose from her braid, and James watched as she tucked it behind her ear.

"Anyway, the crazy guy said it didn't matter if Simon was dead. Once a client hired him, he finished the job." Melinda shuddered. "I'm just glad he's dead and I don't have to worry about Charlotte."

Lucy covered her mouth, looking pale again. James stood, ready to catch her.

"She'll be worried to death. Oh, Mellie. We have to figure out a way to tell her we're alive and well." Lucy wiped her eyes. "Finish telling me what happened."

"It was a car crash. He would have killed me, but the cops arrived and shot him first. I was in a coma for five months. Once I woke, Charlotte helped me get out of the hospital. Then I came to England and went to Blackford. It was in February of 2016."

James wondered what life would be like so many years from now. He was imagining what his own home might look like when something Melinda said made him listen to the two women.

"It was in London I found the painting."

"The painting of my family?"

Melinda nodded.

"Come look." Lucy walked over to the far wall. Curious, James followed.

"This is the one. I wonder how it ended up in a museum?"

Lucy looked thoughtful. "I don't know, but I'm glad it helped you find me."

"It wasn't titled. But I would've known your face anywhere. The colors are so much more vibrant now. How old are your children?" Then Melinda laughed. "I still can't believe you have five kids."

"You can't believe it? How about the fact that I'm forty-four and you're still twenty-six? I'm trying to wrap my head around that."

Lucy touched the painting, tracing each face before sitting down. "The kids range in age from thirteen to nineteen." She looked wistful. "None of them live here. You know when they're young they go foster with another family. And then, as they're older and become knights, they go off to make their own fortune. We see them a few times a year."

"I'm sure you've been a wonderful mother."

They talked for a while longer, and James knew they wanted to discuss him. He stood and made a bow.

"Thank you, Lady Blackford, for extending your hospitality. I must see to the men."

He walked over to Melinda, leaned down, and kissed her. When he turned, he saw Lucy smiling at him. Did she think him good enough for her sister? Or did she only see the beast? James turned on his heel and walked through the doors. As he shut them, he heard the sound of giggling and low feminine voices.

He stopped in the passageway and reached into the pouch at his waist. The ring glittered. Mayhap he was not whole, would never be whole again, but the sapphire reminded him of Melinda, so he slipped it on his finger. For the first time since his injuries, the ring slid over the crooked finger on his left hand.

Chapter Thirty-Four

Melinda and her sister spent the rest of the afternoon and evening talking. She and James were in separate chambers. 'Twas the first night he'd slept apart from her since she'd been sick. He was finding it difficult to be away from her.

The next morning, Renly met James in the bailey. The men were uneasy.

"There are riders in the distance."

"Tell the men to be ready. I will talk with Lord Blackford, but if he will not listen, I will end him."

His captain looked unsure. "Mistress Melinda will be angry if you kill her sister's husband."

"Perhaps you are right, though the man may not give me a choice." What else could James say?

He was still thinking on how to stop William from drawing his sword when Lord Blackford himself rode into the bailey. James watched as William dismounted, counting the number of knights. It would be a fair fight.

He knew the moment William recognized him. The man's face transformed into a look James had seen many times.

"The Red Knight dares send a spy to infiltrate my household?" William roared. "Know you this: the man's blood is on your hands."

James shook his head at Renly and the men, standing there ready for the blow as William stalked over to him.

James heard the sound of Melinda and Lucy's voices. 'Twas the last thing he heard. He returned the blow with one of his own. James admitted that William was a fierce fighter. He took a blow to the side that sent him to his knees. He reached out, grabbed William's foot, and pulled him to the ground. As they rolled across the lists, William gained his feet, unsheathing his sword.

James unsheathed both swords. The clang of steel filled the air. James and Williams spluttered and cursed as a bucket of icy-cold water landed on their heads.

"Bloody hell, woman," William roared at his wife.

"You two are acting like schoolboys, fighting over some stupid toy." Lady Blackford stood with her hands on her hips. James wanted to smile but knew 'twas a bad idea. He only had to look at the two women to tell they were kin.

"You wouldn't listen," Lucy said sweetly.

Melinda put a hand on James' arm. "Talk to him. For my sake."

James bared his teeth. Melinda's tear-filled eyes undid him. He sheathed the blades.

William snarled at James, "'Tis only for my lady,

whoreson. It seems we must talk or incur the wrath of our warrior women. Why are you here, Lord Falconburg?"

"Melinda Merriweather showed up alone, on my lands with no escort." James left the rest unsaid.

Understanding crossed William's face.

"Did you believe her?"

"Not until we arrived here and she found her sister." James looked in the direction of the two women. Both stood there watching them.

William spat blood and sat on a low bench tucked into the corner of the wall. He gestured for James to join him.

As James sat down, a raven landed on the wall above his head. Melinda let out a soft gasp. James looked at her, concerned.

"Is aught amiss, lady?"

"Ravens make me nervous."

"Me too," Lady Blackford said.

The bird cocked its head, as if the creature were listening to them. Then the bloody raven cawed and flew away. Both sisters let out a sigh of relief.

"I was captured by the masked outlaw of the wood."

"And that is what led you here?"

"No, we were already on our way here to see if Lady Blackford was indeed Melinda's sister. On the way, we encountered trouble." James paused, looked to Melinda, saw the look of hope on her face, and turned back to William.

"I heard a tale while I was there. About my family's massacre. Seems we have much to talk about."

William didn't say anything, simply nodded and waited for James to continue. As James watched Melinda and Lucy go inside the hall, he swore.

"I'd rather meet you in the lists again." James sighed. "Seems I needs beg your pardon."

The sound of thunder filled the air. William looked up. "Join me by the fire for a drink?"

"Aye."

William looked over his shoulder.

"I should add another scar to your pretty face."

Just when James thought they had reached an accord, William brought up his disfigurement. He swung, catching William under the chin. Neither man reached for a blade. They used fists, taking out all the anger and hatred they had felt toward each other over the years.

It started to rain. Thunder and lightning filling the sky. And neither man would yield. They hurled insults back and forth. James dealt William a vicious blow to the face. William cursed and unsheathed his sword. James and William fought on through the morning. The garrison knights gathered to watch, calling out advice and hurling insults.

"You fight like a girl, William."

"Mayhap I should cut out your tongue, Jamie boy."

They fought on, neither man willing to concede, both exchanging slurs and blows as the morning gave way to afternoon, then to evening before William said enough. James, drenched in sweat, leaned over, hands on thighs, his bad leg shaking, to catch his breath.

William wiped sweat from his brow.

James walked off the field, then Melinda screamed.

"Look out!"

He turned his head, and that one moment cost him. The knight's sword came down. James heard the sound of the sword striking metal, felt warmth across his hand. With his right hand, he thrust upward with the sword, skewering the man.

William cursed. "My apologies. He was one of Clement's friends. I took him in when he had nowhere else to go."

Melinda ran to him. "Your hands."

Lady Blackford handed Melinda a cloth. "A storm is coming. We need to go in. I'm so sorry, Mellie."

"Not your fault, sis."

"I'll have hot water and clean rags ready when you come in. Hurry. I don't like the look of the sky."

James and William spoke to the men. The knights went to the garrison to take shelter, and William followed Lucy inside. Melinda took the cloth and wiped the blood off his hand.

His ring slid off into her palm. Thunder crashed, making her jump.

"We should go inside, love."

It was as if she didn't hear him. She wiped the blood off

his ring and looked at him, her green eyes glowing in the twilight.

"I've seen this ring before."

"Aye. 'Tis my family ring."

She shook her head. "No. In the future. I found it in the rubble of Falconburg."

The air shifted. Melinda's hair stood out from her head. The wind started to howl and thunder boomed across the sky, shaking the ground. Lightning flashed so close to Melinda, James smelled something burning.

"We must go. Now."

Melinda screamed.

Chapter Thirty-Five

There was no way James had been wearing the ring. She would have noticed it immediately. It was the same ring she'd found in the ruins at Falconburg Castle. Was it possible? Did the ring bring her back? Because when she arrived in the past, it was gone. And now here it was. When did James start wearing it? It was incredibly important she know the answer.

Melinda felt itchy all over. She could hear voices again. Rainbow-colored flashes of light obscured her vision.

And she knew. In this moment she was faced with a choice: stay here in the past with James and Lucy or go back to her own time and her sister Charlotte.

Where was her future? James had kissed her many times, but hadn't said those three little important words. Such small words.

Eight letters in all.

Yet they meant more than an ocean of words. If she

stayed she'd be saying goodbye to Charlotte forever, leaving her sister alone. Melinda loved James. With all her heart. If he didn't love her and she stayed...

She would have Lucy, but would it be enough to balance the loss she would feel every time she saw a man with dark hair? If she went back...she would have Charlotte but lose James and Lucy.

The voices were louder, insistent. Melinda's lungs seemed to be constricting. It was hard to breathe. She had to make a decision or the voices would make it for her.

Melinda closed her eyes, took a deep breath, and made the only choice she could.

Chapter Thirty-Six

Why was Melinda overcome at the sight of his ring? Before his eyes, she started to fade. Panic rose up in James at the thought of losing her. He could see the castle through her form. The storm raged, and James saw the crimson blood, stark against her pale flesh, as she clasped his ring in her hand, blood dripping onto the ground to be washed away by the pounding rain.

She was disappearing before his eyes. He could not lose her. James reached out with both hands, bellowing to the heavens. "I beseech you, do not take my heart. I will gladly remain a beast forever, if only you let her stay."

Chapter Thirty-Seven

Melinda came to. She was in a soft bed in a richly appointed room. It was warm, and the smell of wood smoke and cloves filled the air. A fire crackled in the stone hearth, the mantel carved with flowers and vines. Where was she?

More importantly, *when* was she? She sat up, putting a hand to her head to stop the spinning.

"Please don't let me barf."

When Melinda opened her eyes again, Lucy knelt beside the bed.

"I thought I'd lost you, Mellie."

"The voices told me the choice was mine."

Lucy hugged her so tightly, Melinda squeaked.

"Okay, let me go, you're choking me."

Both of them had tears streaming down their faces. At least she didn't have to worry about looking like a raccoon. No makeup, no mess.

"Saints be, what happened?"

Lucy helped Melinda sit up then moved away from the bed. Melinda looked to James. His hand shook, his normally golden skin pale as hers. He fell to his knees, threw his arms around her waist, and rested his head against her chest.

"Do not ever do such a thing again. I thought I lost you to the future."

She sniffled. He looked wavy through her tears.

"I saw you reach for me through the voices and the lights."

Melinda glanced up to see Lucy quietly leaving the room.

"I kept you from returning home."

Melinda pulled him up to look him in the eye. "You are my home. I wanted to stay."

"You are certain?"

Anger rose within her. She slid off the bed, looking for something to throw. But it was Lucy's room, and she'd feel bad if she broke anything, so she'd settle for yelling.

"Why would a woman as intelligent, kind, and beautiful as you want the beast of Falconburg?"

Melinda turned and punched him in the stomach. It was like hitting rock. "Ouch, that hurt."

His head jerked up.

She would try to make him understand. To see the man she saw so clearly. Put it in words he could relate to.

"Why do you hide in shadow and darkness? Come into the light." Melinda took his face in her hands. "Can't you see? All your life, you have used your looks as a shield. Something to hide your true self behind. Now that shield has been broken, cast into the dirt. And you must rely on what is inside."

She pulled him to the bed, sat beside him, taking his hand in hers.

"As your face is your shield, your actions are your sword and the code you live by. Powerful and sharp. We use what we are given in this life. If something is lost, we use the other tools given us. Can't you see how much others look to you, value you?"

His insecurities had become a crutch. She kicked it out from him.

"I love you. People age, looks fade, and all that remains is what is inside. You are no beast."

Melinda touched his face, tracing the scars with a finger.

"You see me for who I am. Why can't you believe I see you for the man you are?" She held her hands up. "Look at me. I have no title, no money, no lands. You should not want me. I would make a poor match."

A fierce look crossed his face and something flickered in his eyes.

"I would be the most fortunate man in all the realms to have you for my own."

"So why can't you believe I feel the same?"

Chapter Thirty-Eight

James discreetly wiped dust from his eyes. The servants should be dismissed for not doing their duties. He did not weep. 'Twas merely something in his eye. Before him stood a great warrior queen. Melinda loved him for the man he was. Not for his looks or gold. She truly did not see his scars. Only the man.

"I will love you the rest of my life. And beyond. Through whatever lies waiting for us after death. Will you be the Lady of Falconburg? Marry me and make me the happiest man in all the realms."

James pulled her into his arms. As he did, his tunic ripped, the hastily mended garment giving way. He shrugged out of the tunic, turned, and threw it in the fire. Melinda gasped. Doubt crashed down on him.

She walked around him, touching each scar. James stiffened. He knew what his back and chest looked like. A mass of scars. Old white lines crossed with faint pink lines, marred by angry red slashes.

"Do not pull away. You are an amazing warrior and beautiful to me. I do not care how many scars you have. Your skin tells the story of what happened to you on the outside. Others carry their scars on the inside, hidden from everyone but themselves. We all have scars. They make us who we are. I swear I will love you for the rest of my life. And if you will have me, I will marry you, James Rivers."

He gathered her in his arms. A drop of wetness dripped from his face onto her hand. He didn't think he'd cried since his family died. With Melinda he was reborn. A new man. His scars no longer held sway over him.

Chapter Thirty-Nine

Lucy breezed into the solar, a crochet hook and yarn in her hands. "Where are the men?"

"They're out in the stables. James said they needed to discuss horses."

Lucy rolled her eyes. "They'll be out there all day."

Melinda couldn't stop looking at her sister. She was still pretty; it was just startling to see her twenty years older. Melinda kept expecting her to look the same as when she'd disappeared less than a year ago. In time, she'd get used to the change and no longer notice.

"You look good with silver hair."

Lucy touched her hair and laughed. "And the wrinkles around my eyes?"

"Laugh lines are always beautiful."

They sat in front of the fire, eating lunch. While Melinda had less than a year of her life to catch Lucy up on, Lucy shared twenty years worth of news. Talk about a lot happening.

"Thank goodness I saw the merchant at the market wearing one of your scarves. Have you been teaching everyone to crochet?"

"I've taught a few of the serving girls. Just think, my scarf is what brought you to me. Though you would've made your way to Blackford and found me eventually."

"I'm not sure. The man described you—well, let's just say he said you were older and had silver hair. I would have thought it was someone else."

"You were going to call me old. Go ahead and say it."

"It's a lot to take in."

"Who would've ever thought we'd be living in a castle?"

"I still can't believe you have five children. And went through childbirth at home, not in a hospital. And without drugs."

"At the time I couldn't believe it either. You should have heard me screaming. But if I were back home, I would've been one of those women other pregnant women hated. All of my pregnancies were easy. I was sick for the first month and that was it. Otherwise I felt great. When I went into labor, the midwife came, I pushed five or six times, and out came baby."

"Some of those pregnant woman, like that awful Caroline Smith with the fake boobs, would've strung you up by your toes."

Lucy's eyes filled with tears. "What are we going to do about Charlotte? By now she's gotten the news you're missing or presumed dead. She'll think she's lost us both, and she doesn't even have Aunt Pittypat anymore."

"She knows about the painting. I told her when I found it. We can hide a letter, but if we do, we need to make sure we seal it in wax or something to protect it."

"I'm so happy you're here, Mellie. The only thing that would make me happier would be if Charlotte were here too. Could you see her in medieval England?"

"She'd have everyone doing yoga at sunrise, meditating in the afternoon, and giving up meat."

"I'm not sure she'd survive without her high-powered blender."

They laughed, and Melinda felt her throat close up. She'd been so lost without her sister, missed her so very much. It was wonderful to be reunited, and yet bittersweet, for now she and Charlotte were separated by an ocean of time. It was hard to let go.

"So...what's the deal with James?"

Melinda scooted her chair closer to Lucy. She leaned in, and Lucy leaned in too, so close their heads almost touched.

"He's wonderful. Actually asks what I think. Listens."

"I always hated that about Carl. It was like he couldn't see past your looks. What happened to James?"

"He's enemies with some family named Bolton in the south. He said it happened during a battle. From how awful the scars are, I think they did it on purpose."

"He's still handsome."

"The scars don't bother me at all. Half the time I don't even notice them." She looked up to see Lucy looking at her, a skeptical look on her face.

"Really. I see him for who he is on the inside. A good man with a strong personal code. Someone who cares about me as a person, not an object or possession. And someone who would risk everything to save me. I love him with all my heart."

She told Lucy about James saving her from bandits and saving her from almost drowning. And then she told Lucy how she'd saved him.

"You should've seen his face when I made him do a piggyback. He said he was humiliated."

"That huge man on your back? How did you even take a step? He must outweigh you by a hundred pounds."

She and Lucy burst into giggles.

"I felt like I had an elephant on my back. That man is solid muscle. But I knew I had to get him out of there. So I put one foot in front of the other and tried to focus on not falling over. Maybe the core exercises Charlotte made me learn helped."

Lucy touched her stomach. "I do planks every morning, but never when the servants are around. William would have stomped and bellowed around for a week if he'd been saved by a woman."

"James was so angry at first. I think his pride was damaged more than anything else. He'd never been rescued by a woman before." She snorted. "I don't think he'd ever been rescued, period."

"They definitely believe the whole 'me man, you woman' thing."

She and Lucy talked through the afternoon, so happy to

be together again. One of the servants knocked on the door.

"Lady Blackford? Lord Blackford is in the hall with Lord Falconburg and the men."

"We will join them presently."

Lucy put the crochet away in a basket by her feet. "We better go down before they start gnawing on the tables."

Melinda took Lucy's arm in hers. "I'm starved. What's for dinner?"

"I'm not sure. We've been so busy catching up, I told cook to come up with whatever. After dinner, we need to put our heads together and write down what we know about traveling through time. Charlotte needs to know. Anything that can help her get back to us."

"But we have to be really careful. We don't want the wrong people finding a letter. Think of all the havoc someone could cause by coming back and assassinating a king."

"Let's just hope Charlotte doesn't come back more than twenty years from now. I'll be a granny or dead by then."

"No you won't. Lucy Merriweather, you are to stay around for a very long time. I didn't travel over seven hundred years so you could join Aunt Pittypat in the great beyond. I forbid it."

Melinda clapped a hand over her mouth. "What if Charlotte comes back and it's before we're here?"

"Mellie, don't even think it."

Chapter Forty

After dinner, the men remained in the hall drinking and talking. Melinda followed Lucy into the solar.

"Dinner was delicious."

"Thank goodness merchants come through frequently with spices. They're ghastly expensive, but William has loads of money and doesn't care how much I spend. He's grown quite accustomed to some of the dishes I've made."

"Your fried chicken rocks. Don't you worry about changing history?"

"For a long time I did. Then I decided the things I do are so small it doesn't matter. At least, that's what I hope."

Lucy chuckled.

"William said James is even richer than we are."

"I don't care. Although I'm glad I didn't come back and end up with a peasant. They have a hard life."

"Money always makes things easier, no matter what time you live in. I didn't care much about money in our time. But here, it can make your life comfortable, and I've grown used to it."

"What do you remember about traveling through time?"

Lucy's face turned pale.

"There was a storm. I remember the lightning. Of course, you have to remember I was drugged, so everything seemed like I was in a movie."

Lucy's hand trembled as she took a drink.

"There was also a raven. I swear I saw the same raven a hundred times before and after I traveled through time."

"I've seen a raven too. Lots of times. I believe he helped me find your letter."

"What's the deal with the bird?"

"I have no idea," Melinda said. "But he's connected to all of this."

"I also remember blood. There was a strange stain on the battlements of the castle. At first I thought it was some kind of hole in the wall. I grabbed it to try to keep Simon from throwing me over the wall."

Melinda put a hand on her sister's knee. "I'm glad he's dead. He was a horrible person."

"Part of the Merriweather curse. Bad judgment in men, and a terrible sense of direction."

"You're not kidding. When I left Falconburg, I would've

ended up in Scotland if James hadn't found me."

"You know, I think the blood is the final piece of the puzzle. The stain on the wall. It was my blood. I thought it was William's all along, but it wasn't. It was mine. When his frenemy Clement stabbed me, I saw my blood on the wall, and that's when the lightning and everything came together at once. I knew I had the choice whether to stay or go. I made my choice, and at the same time William pulled me back."

Melinda vibrated with excitement.

"Something similar happened to me. I found a ring. It had a nick in the band. When I put it on, I cut my thumb and bled. There was a terrible storm. Lightning struck so close to me I thought I was going to fry. When I woke up, I was in the past. And then a few days ago, when James and William had their little tiff, I saw the same ring on James' hand. When that man tried to kill James and cut his hand, that's when I knew..."

Lucy finished the thought: "So we have to have all three. The raven, the storm, blood, and the object seems to be optional."

"We have to figure out how to leave a message for Charlotte without telling the whole world."

Chapter Forty-One

Present Day—Deep in the Carpathian Mountains

Charlotte woke coughing. Smoke filled the room and she could see flames. The tiny wooden building was on fire. She couldn't believe it. The man who'd tried to kill Melinda, put her in a coma, was dead. This was a simple accident, nothing more.

She was deep in the Carpathian Mountains, where she'd run to get away from all the craziness. On her hands and knees, Charlotte crawled for the door. It wouldn't open. Something was blocking it from the other side. She grabbed one of the scarves Lucy had made her and held it to her mouth to keep the smoke from filling her lungs. As she crawled in the opposite direction, she searched for the window. It was her only way out.

The sound of a raven calling came from her left. The bird seemed to be leading her to safety. Charlotte pushed up the window and rolled over the edge, landing in the snow. She breathed in, coughing, her battered lungs burning.

Charlotte sat in the internet cafe and checked her email. Her friend Jake was housesitting and said the police were trying to get in touch with her. When she called, the nice officer informed her Melinda had taken her own life.

Even though she knew there was no way both of her sisters had tried to kill themselves, Charlotte let the tears fall. She knew in her heart there was no way both of them had fallen to their deaths. But she didn't say any of this to the officer. She thanked him for telling her and ended the call, sniffling and blowing her nose.

There were enough bizarre happenings in this small town to make Charlotte certain there was more to this world than we could see and feel.

She would visit the one person she thought could give her some insight. The oldest woman in the village. Marielle was rumored to have the sight. Maybe she could tell Charlotte what had happened to Lucy and Melinda. She snorted. It wasn't like the cops had a clue.

Charlotte knocked on the bright blue door. Marielle opened the door, beckoning her in.

"I've been expecting you."

"Melinda is dead. At least, that's what the police officer

told me. He said she was visiting some castle ruin and jumped to her death out of grief. I know my sister. She would not kill herself."

Charlotte wiped the tears from her eyes and blew her nose. She met the gypsy woman's wise eyes.

"Can you please tell me what happened to my sisters?"

The woman shuffled a worn deck of tarot cards. She laid them out in three rows of seven, from left to right.

"The top row is your past. The center row the present. And the bottom row is your future."

Marielle looked at the cards for a long time.

"You will find your sisters in England. But not this England."

"Melinda saw a painting in London. She swore it was of our sister Lucy. It was painted during the fourteenth century. Do you mean I can actually go back in time?"

"What is time? Time does not flow in a line. It is a circle. There are many possibilities if only you listen."

The woman gathered up the cards and put them away. She took Charlotte's hands in hers, looking at her palms.

"Be wary, child. Great danger awaits you. Look for the raven. He will guide your path. And the unicorn will bring great change to your life. Be ready."

Unicorns? Charlotte believed in a lot of things, things others called New Age or ridiculous. But even she didn't believe in unicorns.

"Thank you, Marielle. It's time for me to leave. To go home and prepare."

The little old gypsy lady kissed her on each cheek.

"Be strong, Charlotte. Your destiny awaits, if you have the courage to take it."

If Lucy had gone back in time, did the gypsy mean Melinda had found a way to go back too? Charlotte needed to research and prepare. She didn't know how she could go back, only that she must.

She grabbed her meager belongings and stuffed them into the back of the waiting taxi. While it made more sense to fly to England from Romania, she needed to go back to Holden Beach first. Tie up loose ends. Say goodbye to her childhood home and figure out a plan. Her sisters might call her flighty and free-spirited, but she had a knack for figuring things out.

She didn't have a will, and there was the house and cars to deal with. Charlotte pulled out a small notebook from her bag and started a list. The fact that Lucy never returned and now Melinda was missing told Charlotte once you ended up in the past, you were stuck. So she would take care of what she needed to and then catch a flight to England. And somehow she would find a way to travel through time and find her sisters. Though what if they ended up in different times?

"No!"

"Miss?"

"Sorry. I was talking to myself."

The driver nodded and went back to humming to himself. Lucy and Melinda had to be together. Fate couldn't be so cruel.

Chapter Forty-Two

Holden Beach, North Carolina

A month had passed since Charlotte returned home to Holden Beach. She was completely healed from the burns on her arms and legs from the fire. Thanks to an old recipe of Aunt Pittypat's, she wouldn't scar.

Charlotte noticed her finger shaking as she switched off the iPad. Melinda Merriweather, American, apparent suicide due to grief over losing her sister, who died almost a year ago. Both sisters drowned and were presumed lost at sea.

Two of her sisters go to England and are presumed dead or missing? Something smelled worse than a pot of collards left on the stove for two days and two nights.

Why hadn't she listened to Melinda? Gone with her? And what was with the Brits wanting to kill all three of them? She'd barely escaped the fire. Had come to believe someone was still after her. Why?

There had to be a reason. Charlotte jumped on her bike and rode to the local bookstore. Inside she perused the stacks. She bought books on the history of England, particularly those with a focus on the fourteenth century. Books on field medicine, plants, and herbs. Oh, and let's not forget books on witchcraft and New Age ideas. As she took the huge stack up to the checkout, the cute guy wearing glasses flirted with her.

"Wow, that's a lot of information. Are you studying for a class?"

"You could say that. I'm going to England for vacation, so I thought it would be fun to visit a few castles."

He picked up the book on field medicine. "Well, unless you're planning to start a war while you're there, I don't think you'll need this one."

"It's always good to broaden your horizons, don't you think?"

Charlotte collected her purchases, filling up the basket on the bike. One thing to check off her list. While she hated taking any more time before she went to England, she felt it was important to be prepared. Her flight left two weeks from today. That should give her enough time to read through the books and make notes. She was a firm believer in notes.

As Charlotte sat outside on the deck overlooking the ocean, she opened the leather-bound journal she'd purchased in the store. It was expensive compared to the cheapie notebooks she usually bought. But it looked old, so it shouldn't arouse suspicion if anyone saw it.

She planned to fill it with anything she might need during her journey. Moments in history, various plants used for healing, and, of course, Aunt Pittypat's famous recipes. All of them would go in the journal. Charlotte had a friend who might be able to get her antibiotics. That seemed like the one thing she wanted to take back with her.

A solar charger and phone so she could play music would be nice, but she decided against it. She didn't know why, but she was afraid to have too many modern things with her when she tried to go back in time.

Thanks to the power of the internet, she'd done most of her research online. There were a group of history buffs in Northern England she planned meet up with. They'd been emailing back and forth. One of the guys said he'd teach her how to use a knife. He didn't think she would have long enough for him to teach her to use a sword. That was fine. One weapon would do.

No way could she take a knife on the plane. She'd buy an antique when she arrived. Flying into London would be perfect. Charlotte could scour some of the shops looking for the rest of what she needed. Things like a cloak and clothes to help her blend in. She could sew reasonably well, so she planned to add pockets to anything that didn't come with.

As she ate a slice of pizza, Charlotte opened the first book and began reading.

Books by Cynthia Luhrs
Listed in the correct reading order

A JIG THE PIG ADVENTURE (Children's Picture Books)
Beware the Woods
I am NOT a Chicken!

MERRIWEATHER SISTERS TIME TRAVEL
A Knight to Remember
Knight Moves
Lonely is the Knight - February 2016

THE SHADOW WALKER GHOST SERIES
Lost in Shadow
Desired by Shadow
Iced in Shadow
Reborn in Shadow
Born in Shadow
Embraced by Shadow

Want More?

Thank you for reading my book. If you enjoyed it, please consider writing a few words in a review to help others discover the Merriweather books. Let me know your thoughts. I love to hear from my readers. To find out when there's a new book release, please visit my website http://cluhrs.com/ and sign up for my newsletter. Want to drop me a line? Please LIKE my page on Facebook. Love connecting with all of my readers because without you, none of this would be possible. http://www.facebook.com/cynthialuhrsauthor

P.S. Prefer another form of social media? You'll find links to all my social media sites there.

Thank you!

Mailing List

Subscribe to Cynthia's Mailing List http://cluhrs.com/connect/ to receive exclusive updates from Cynthia Luhrs and to be the first to get instant access to cover releases, chapter excerpts, and win great prizes!

About the Author

Cynthia Luhrs is the author of the ghostly Shadow Walker novels and the Merriweather Sisters Time Travel Romance novels set in medieval England. Her idea of a perfect day is no interruptions and the freedom to live in her head all day, writing to her heart's content, a glass of sweet tea next to her as she creates the next book. Of course her tiger cats frequently disrupt this oasis of serenity.

CPSIA information can be obtained
at www.ICGtesting.com
Printed in the USA
LVOW04s0206260916

506162LV00044B/2716/P

9 781519 295491